D0840901

Sherlock Holmes and the Adventure of the Fallen Soufflé

by

David MacGregor

First edition published in 2021
© Copyright 2021
David MacGregor

The right of David MacGregor to be identified as the author of
this work has been asserted by him in accordance with the
Copyright, Designs and Patents Act 1998.

All rights reserved. No reproduction, copy or transmission of
this publication may be made without express prior written
permission. No paragraph of this publication may be
reproduced, copied or transmitted except with express prior
written permission or in accordance with the provisions of the
Copyright Act 1956 (as amended). Any person who commits
any unauthorised act in relation to this publication may be liable
to criminal prosecution and civil claims for damage.

All characters appearing in this work are fictitious. Any
resemblance to real persons, living or dead, is purely
coincidental. The opinions expressed herein are those of the
author and not of MX Publishing.

Paperback ISBN 978-1-78705-714-2
ePub ISBN 978-1-78705-715-9
PDF ISBN 978-1-78705-716-6

Published by Orange Pip Books
335 Princess Park Manor, Royal Drive,
London, N11 3GX
www.orangepipbooks.com

Cover design by Brian Belanger

For Torin

Acknowledgments

This story, along with its companion pieces, "Sherlock Holmes and the Adventure of the Elusive Ear" and "Sherlock Holmes and the Adventure of the Ghost Machine," began life as a play at The Purple Rose Theatre Company in Chelsea, Michigan. First and foremost, my eternal thanks goes to my friend and colleague Guy Sanville, who directed "Elusive Ear," and always pushes me to make the story better. My gratitude also goes toward the dozens of talented and highly skilled collaborators who made these plays successful. And of course, my thanks to actor, playwright, composer, and musician Jeff Daniels for founding The Purple Rose Theatre Company in 1991 and providing a home for innumerable artists.

Special thanks goes to Hope Shangle, who offered an attentive ear and thoughtful insights over coffee and pastries, then volunteered her considerable web wizard talents as needed. Thanks also to the Amateur Mendicant Society of Detroit and Holmesian guru Howard Ostrom, whose enthusiasm for this new version of Sherlock Holmes was deeply appreciated. My brother Iain MacGregor and good friend Peter Morris were kind enough to cast a careful eye over the text, and I am extremely grateful to Steve Emecz, Richard Ryan, and the team at MX Publishing for gracefully ushering these stories into a different medium and giving them an entirely new audience.

Finally, a deep and heartfelt bow to Sir Arthur Conan Doyle for creating, as Vincent Starrett poetically expressed it, "two men of note who never lived and so can never die."

Contents

Introduction

Bertie is dead. Or, to put a more distinguished gloss on it, Edward VII, King of England and Emperor of India, has passed on to a better place than this. Or not. As much as I would like it to be the former, I fear that it may be the latter due to his disgraceful young adulthood and dissolute middle age. Like many of my fellow British citizens, prior to his arrival at 221B seeking the help of Sherlock Holmes, I was aware that Bertie appeared to have more than his fair share of royal indiscretions and scandals, but it was only after meeting him in person that I became aware of just what an insufferable lout His Royal Highness really was.

However, at that point in time he was still the Prince of Wales, and it must be said that he managed to redeem himself to a considerable extent once he became King. Personally, I don't doubt for a moment that his experiences in this case were a large contributing factor in his rehabilitation. But I'm getting ahead of myself. Bertie's death is relevant to the extent that I now feel free to tell the remarkable story of "The Adventure of the Fallen Soufflé."

Not that I plan on publishing it while I am still alive, of course. No, thank you. The last thing I need in my dotage is the wrath of the royal family and the gutter press breathing down my neck for more and more salacious details. So, just as I related the story of "The Adventure of the Elusive Ear" and consigned it to my despatch box at Cox and Company for future generations, I shall do precisely the same thing with this tale. The same fate is in store for yet another story, "The Adventure of the Ghost Machine," which is currently in preparation. I hope that all three tales will eventually see the light of day so as to give the reading public a fuller understanding of my friend Sherlock Holmes, but should they end up being consigned to the flames by some thickheaded Philistine, then so be it.

By that point I shall be long past caring. Bearing that in mind, and in keeping with the level of candour that I allowed myself in "Elusive Ear," this account will not be confined by the prim and proper style insisted upon by my publisher George Newnes in "The Strand Magazine," where the Sherlock Holmes adventures first appeared. His insistence on wholesome stories with wholesome language was taken a bit too far in my opinion, and I always resented it when he took up his editing pen and changed my "lost soul in hell" to "lost soul in torment" or transformed my "devils" into "fiends." But old George isn't with us anymore either, having passed away a month after Bertie, and so I propose to give my readers a fuller and more realistic portrait of not only Sherlock Holmes, but of all the characters associated with this case.

First, a little housekeeping is in order to set the scene, as it were. At the time this case took place, our cosy living arrangements at 221B Baker Street consisted of myself, Sherlock Holmes, and his lover, Irene Adler. Yes, you read that correctly. Following the conclusion of "A Scandal in Bohemia," Miss Adler had taken up residence with us for the simple reason that she and Holmes were madly in love with one another. As much as I would like to claim that I gracefully adapted to these new living arrangements with no complaint, that would not be entirely true.

In point of fact, I was stunned, baffled, and more than a little bit outraged. For those readers not familiar with our encounter with Miss Adler in "A Scandal in Bohemia," let me summarise by saying that she was an opera-singing American adventuress who came to the attention of Sherlock Holmes because she was blackmailing the King of Bohemia. In other words, scarcely the sort of individual that I had ever imagined having as a roommate.

However, once she and Holmes laid eyes on one other, that was that. Their attraction to one another was as instantaneous as it was profound. Even they were a bit stunned by their feelings. During the course of their respective lifetimes they had each built up what they had assumed was an impenetrable fortress around their hearts. This was not only for their own protection, but also for the protection of the general public.

Possessed of unique, powerful, idiosyncratic personalities, they recognised early on that they were not particularly well suited to lives of domestic tranquility with a loving (or at least tolerant) partner. Rather, like Da Vinci or Isaac Newton, they would throw all of their intellect and passion into their work. This both Miss Adler and Holmes had done, up until the day they met. At first they had sparred with one another, both emotionally and intellectually, fully expecting that the other person would quite sensibly flee for the hills at some point. But that never happened. Instead, each flurry of words or exchange of ideas pulled them closer and closer, until inevitably, they stopped fighting against it, and I arrived home one evening to find Miss Adler unpacking all of her belongings with the eager assistance of Holmes.

As the writer and narrator of the incredibly popular Sherlock Holmes stories in "The Strand Magazine," this put me in a bit of a quandary, to put it mildly. The Sherlock Holmes beloved by his readers was a confirmed bachelor. As was I. True, I had concocted a rather ridiculous romance and marriage between Mary Morstan and myself in the second Sherlock Holmes novel,

3

"The Sign of the Four," but that was done solely with the rather cynical aim of attracting more female readers and had no basis in reality whatsoever.

Once the Sherlock Holmes stories became a national sensation in "The Strand," I gratefully jettisoned my "wife" by killing her off, leaving Holmes and I as two adventuring bachelors solving bizarre and fascinating mysteries together. What could be better than that? The police and clients could arrive at any hour with outlandish crimes to relate, Holmes and I could dash off to an opium den or into the English countryside at a moment's notice, and there were no domestic concerns whatsoever. And then Miss Adler came along.

My first instinct (and in retrospect, I can't say that I am proud of this) was to kill her off as well. This was accomplished at the end of "A Scandal in Bohemia," where I referred to her as "the late Irene Adler, of dubious and questionable memory." I knew very well that the British reading public wouldn't stand for Sherlock Holmes being in love or taking up residence with an unmarried woman, so the simplest solution seemed to be her untimely demise. Still, I was then faced with the very real Miss Adler who now shared our rooms.

Somehow, I had to explain her presence whenever new clients arrived, and after several sleepless nights I arrived at a most elegant solution. Miss Adler would be our housekeeper, the widowed "Mrs. Hudson." I will confess that it was with a certain amount of trepidation that I broached this plan to Miss Adler and Holmes, but to my considerable relief, they both took to it immediately. Holmes saw the practicality of it, and Miss Adler, an inveterate performer, was delighted at the prospect of playing a character. In fact, in the early days of this little charade, she had given Mrs. Hudson a rather alarming Cockney accent, although that had been dropped from her repertoire as of late.

My consternation at having Miss Adler living with us abated soon enough, in large part because I quickly came to appreciate her own very considerable intellect and abilities. Widely read, a superb fencer, and with an almost instinctive facility for foreign languages, she and Holmes complemented one another wonderfully, with the added benefit that her presence discouraged Holmes from becoming lazy and not giving his full attention to a case, as with "The Adventure of the Yellow Face." She had a similar salutary effect on Holmes' drug use, as in the past he had typically reached for the cocaine needle when he was bored, and life with Miss Adler was anything but boring.

Moreover, as the weeks and months passed, I realised I had an ally in Miss Adler, especially when Holmes was feeling restless and disputatious. She had a neat and precise way of puncturing his pretensions, and she was especially useful when it came to getting Holmes out of the room so I could get a bit of writing done without having to listen to his critical comments.

In summation, it is fair to say that while Miss Adler and I may have begun our association as wary housemates, over time we had become genuinely fond of one another, and it was now impossible to conceive of a more ideal living arrangement than the one we had. So it was that on the day this particular adventure began, I was quite happily putting together a traditional English breakfast for Miss Adler in celebration of her birthday.

(Editor's Note: In the original Sherlock Holmes stories, astute historians noted occasional factual errors and timeline discrepancies, which were invariably put down to the unreliability of Dr. Watson. This tendency did not diminish as the good Doctor entered his later years, but it does not detract in any meaningful way from the pleasure to be had in this long-hidden tale from the annals of Sherlock Holmes.)

Chapter One
A Traditional English Breakfast

London: June 21, 1897.

I enjoy cooking. Not on a regular basis, of course, but on special occasions I take a certain pleasure in puttering about the kitchen mixing ingredients, making sure the heat is just right, and sampling the results as I go along. Today, Miss Adler's birthday, was just such an occasion. As an Englishman, I had somehow reached adulthood assuming that everyone had access to the same fine fare that I was used to consuming on a regular basis, whether it be a fresh Dover sole or a thick slice of Beef Wellington, and perhaps a nice trifle for dessert, followed by port and cigars.

Growing older and wiser, I began to realise that this was not necessarily identical to menus in Japan or America, and then growing even more old and more wise, had the dawning realisation that English cuisine was not exactly revered around the world. This, in truth, came as a bit of a shock to me, but it was not an exaggeration. The French in particular were absolutely insufferable when it came to comparing their cuisine to that of England, and I recall a particularly unpleasant evening at the Albemarle Club being lectured by a weedy-looking Frenchman about Hollandaise sauce, of all things.

So it was that last week, when Holmes reminded me that Miss Adler's birthday was approaching, I immediately took to considering what sort of gift I could get her. For me, presents fall into two categories, either things or experiences. Miss Adler was far too cosmopolitan a woman to be caught up in the acquisition of material possessions, so I determined that my present to her would have to be some kind of experience. But what experience, precisely?

There was always a concert or play, of course, but that would simply entail buying a ticket to the event, and I knew that she would rather go to either one of those with Holmes. I briefly flirted with the idea of taking her to a bare-knuckle boxing match featuring the peerless Jem Mace, but upon reflection realised that was more of a present for me than for Miss Adler. When I landed upon the idea of making her a meal, I knew instantly I had found my answer. Of course, Holmes would probably take her to Simpson's for dinner, and lunch was always an uncertain proposition if we had a case at hand, so logic dictated that a traditional English breakfast would be just the thing to start her day and open her eyes to all the delights of British cuisine.

I had arisen early, fussed over every little particular, and now, putting the finishing touches on my creation, I thoughtfully put a cloche over the plate to keep the dish warm and to heighten the surprise factor. After a brief but fruitless hunt around the kitchen for a birthday candle, I made my way up the stairs, where I knew Miss Adler was waiting, no doubt in hungry anticipation. At the last moment an inspired idea came to me, a snatch of a new song I had heard wafting out of a tenement house only last week, and being a simple little ditty, I launched into it as I opened the door to our rooms.

"Happy birthday to you!
Happy birthday to you!
Happy birthday, Miss Adler!
Happy birthday to you!"

With that, I placed the covered dish before Miss Adler, who was seated at our breakfast table with what I must say appeared to be a look of apprehension and concern on her face. Glancing at Holmes, I got the distinct impression that he was struggling not to burst out laughing, and it was clear that some kind of very peculiar conversation had been taking place just before my arrival. As this was not exactly an unprecedented event, it didn't bother me in the slightest. Perhaps it would be made clear to me or perhaps not, but at the moment I had a more pressing concern on my mind.

"And here you are, Miss Adler!" I announced. "As promised, a traditional English breakfast! A very happy birthday to you!"

With that, I removed the cloche and was gratified to see an expression of complete and utter astonishment on Miss Adler's face. She then proceeded to look at the dish from a number of different angles, taking it all in. I had gone to considerable pains in terms of plating the dish, striving for what I hoped was a rather pleasing geometrical arrangement, rather than simply throwing the food on the plate in a slapdash fashion. I glanced at Holmes, who was nodding encouragingly, and finally, Miss Adler looked up at me, and after a moment's hesitation asked, "What is it?"

Not entirely certain which portion of the breakfast she was referring to, I was forced to ask, "What's what?"

"This brown thing."

"It's a kipper!" I replied, surprised that she had never seen one before. As she picked it up by its tail, she looked to Holmes for explanation, which he happily provided.

"An entire herring, my dear. Invariably split from head to tail along the dorsal ridge, gutted, salted, and smoked over oak."

"It's a salty fish with the tail and bones?" asked Miss Adler.

"Quite right!" I confirmed. "Very traditional."

Miss Adler pointed to her plate. "And these smaller brown things?"

"Kidneys!" I replied, beginning to realise that Miss Adler was perhaps not quite as cosmopolitan a woman as I had imagined.

"No, they're not," she answered.

"I assure you they are. Quite fresh too! Just picked them up yesterday from Smithfield's."

"You know what you should do, Watson?" offered Holmes. "In your efforts to introduce Irene to all the delights of British cuisine, for her next birthday you should prepare a traditional Scottish breakfast."

"Capital idea! Black pudding!" I turned to Miss Adler. "That will put some hair on your chest! Metaphorically speaking, of course."

"What in God's name is black pudding?"

"Sausage made from pig's blood, a little oatmeal, and various spices," explained Holmes. "Typically fried in its own skin, but it can also be baked or boiled, depending on the preference of the gourmet enjoying it."

"It's absolutely delicious!" I enthused. "And of course, quite traditional."

At this, an odd sound emerged from Holmes, something like a laugh being choked back. I was also aware that Miss Adler had yet to pick up any utensils to sample her breakfast and it was quite clear that something was going on between them.

"All right, out with it," I began. "What have I missed?"

"Nothing, old fellow! Nothing at all," replied Holmes. "But coincidentally enough, just before you arrived bearing your sumptuous breakfast feast, Irene made a rather pretty little speech about her feelings on 'tradition,' didn't you, my dear?"

"Oh really?" I was immediately intrigued. "Well, I don't want your breakfast to get cold, but I would be fascinated to hear the thoughts of an American, Miss Adler. Perhaps you can tell me while you eat."

I brought out my notebook, as I always appreciated her insights on British customs. Hailing from New Jersey, of all places, she quite often offered up rather perceptive observations regarding this or that aspect of British culture that I had always taken for granted. However, in this particular instance, rather than launching immediately into a disquisition on the subject of "tradition," she had fixed Holmes with a rather strange expression.

"Explain to me what I see in you again."

"Everything," Holmes replied, with his typical cocksure manner. "And that would, of course, be the sorriest fate ever bestowed upon a woman, were it not for the fact that you know quite well the feeling is mutual. Now then, do share with the good doctor your thoughts on 'tradition.' He has his notebook out, after all."

At that, Miss Adler picked up her fork and began moving a piece of kidney around on her plate, apparently gathering her thoughts.

"'Traditional...'" began Miss Adler, "...is the single most terrifying word in the English language. Because inevitably, what does that mean? It means something ghastly, something truly horrible, that somehow, for some reason, has managed to remain in existence, so that after enough years have passed it's looked upon as beloved and revered, and it becomes a perverse duty to enter into this elaborate lie that everyone agrees on about how wonderful the tradition is."

I was writing all this down as quickly as possible, anxious to quote her correctly, so I didn't initially have time to consider the meaning behind her words. However, once I had put a period at the end of the sentence and looked back over it to make sure I had it right, it began to dawn on me that Miss Adler and I regarded the concept of "tradition" in somewhat different lights. However, before I had time to question her, our attention was drawn by the sound of shouting and police whistles in the street.

A moment later, our downstairs door opened with a crash, heavy footsteps pounded up the stairs, and into the room burst a man absolutely crazed with fear. He was middle-aged, with an enormous white moustache, wore a white chef's jacket, had a toque on his head, and to my considerable alarm brandished a large meat cleaver as he shouted the word, "Ruined!"

He thereupon rushed to the window to look out onto Baker Street as the police whistles and shouting drew nearer, then came back to the centre of the room clearly overcome with emotion, whispered the word "ruined" again, and promptly fainted dead to the floor. Outside, the police whistles passed directly beneath our window and then gradually faded away as the constables ran past. Holmes, Miss Adler, and I all looked at one another, until Holmes pointed out the readily obvious.

"I say, that's certainly livened up our morning."

I walked over to the still form of our surprise visitor to make sure he was still breathing. "Who the devil is he?"

"No idea," replied Holmes, "but perhaps a touch of brandy for our guest will bring him around."

As I moved to get a glass of brandy from the sideboard, both Holmes and Miss Adler examined the man closely. Holmes picked up the cleaver, running his eyes across it.

"Obviously a cook or chef of some kind," I offered.

"Indeed," agreed Holmes. "The capital letter K stamped into the blade of his cleaver indicates that it was manufactured by the French company Sabatier, which would naturally suggest a French chef, but the worn boots, which were made by Mr. John Branch of Bethnal Green Road, tell us he has been living in London for some time. Judging by the peculiar combination of tar and gravel adhering to his left instep, he either works or resides near Covent Garden, where roadwork is currently being performed. Irene, is there anything you would add to shed some light on this gentleman's identity?"

"Just one small detail," answered Miss Adler. "His name is Auguste Escoffier, and he is the most celebrated chef in the world. Inventor of the *bombe Néro* and *fraises à la Sarah Bernhardt*, he is the head chef at London's most glittering restaurant, The Savoy Hotel."

As I arrived with the brandy and poured a small amount into the chef's mouth, Holmes looked at Miss Adler in shock. "Marvellous, my dear! But how on earth—"

It was at that moment that our guest regained consciousness, choking a little on the brandy as he gazed up at us with the eyes of a hunted animal, before squinting in confusion as he looked at Miss Adler as if she were a ghost.

"Irene?"

"Auguste. How nice to see you."

"But you are dead!"

"Apparently not."

With that, Escoffier got to his feet, suddenly remembering the frantic events that had brought him to our rooms. He rushed to the window, looking up and down the now quiet street.

"Looking for something, Mr. Escoffier?" asked Holmes.

"No, no! I thought that...but perhaps I was mistaken." Gathering his wits with every passing moment, Escoffier smiled broadly at Miss Adler and then kissed her on both cheeks.

"Irene! How wonderful that you are alive! But I do not understand. I came to see Mr. Sherlock Holmes. How is it that you are here?"

"There is actually a very simple explanation for that," returned Miss Adler. "Mr. Holmes is my lover. Has been ever since the affair that Dr. Watson memorably referred to as 'A Scandal in Bohemia' in 'The Strand Magazine.'"

"Yes! Which is the story that said you are dead!"

"As you are well aware Auguste, at the time I was running in the dubious circles of society's best and brightest and had somehow managed to make several powerful enemies. I judged it in my best interest to disappear for a little while. Dr. Watson has been gracious enough to explain my presence here by casting me in the stories as Mrs. Hudson, the housekeeper of the celebrated Sherlock Holmes."

"And you say he is your lover? I find that very difficult to believe. Sherlock Holmes, he does not like the women, *n'est-ce pas?*"

"I find this one tolerable from time to time," offered Holmes with a wry smile.

"Which, if I might translate for you, Auguste, means that he adores me with every fibre of his being."

"That I do."

Should Escoffier have had any suspicion that this was some kind of elaborate charade concocted by Holmes and Miss Adler, all doubts would have been dispelled from his mind simply from the manner in which Holmes and Miss Adler now looked at one another. Only a blind man could not have seen that these were two people very much in love.

"Well, well, well!" Escoffier seemed highly pleased to be let in on this little secret, twirling his moustache with an elegant flourish. "You do have a way with the men, Irene. I cannot deny that. This will make for some delicious gossip in the kitchen."

"I wouldn't recommend it," replied Miss Adler. "That would displease Mr. Holmes, and people who displease Mr. Holmes have a tendency to plunge to their deaths from waterfalls."

"You mean, as with the late Professor Moriarty? But that was a fair fight, yes? And according to Dr. Watson's story, it was Moriarty who attacked Mr. Holmes."

Hearing my name, I looked up from my notebook. "To be perfectly candid, I wasn't actually there. But Holmes' word is good enough for me."

I directed a glance at Holmes, who studiously avoided my gaze. Like many of my readers, I have long wondered what precisely happened between Holmes and Professor Moriarty at the Reichenbach Falls, but it was not a topic that Holmes relished discussing. Upon his return from his supposed death (or "hiatus" as I like to think of it), he had made a brief statement to me regarding how events unfolded, along the lines that I subsequently related in "The Adventure of the Empty House." Moriarty had lured Holmes to the precipice of the Falls, a struggle had ensued, with Moriarty ultimately plunging to his death and Holmes going into hiding for three years.

That was the bare bones of it, and despite the fact that I had raised the topic a number of times in the ensuing years, Holmes was disinclined to comment further. Privately, I will confess that I suspect Holmes' version of events may not be entirely in keeping with the facts. Why on earth would an elderly Professor of Mathematics imagine that he could physically overcome a man like Sherlock Holmes? It was true that I exaggerated a few of Holmes' abilities in my stories for effect, but Professor Moriarty was intelligent enough to know that his odds of surviving a physical altercation with Holmes were slight at best. It was a mystery, to be sure, and not one that Holmes planned on solving for me.

"Then there was Dr. Grimesby Roylott," offered Miss Adler, "who died after being bitten by a swamp adder in 'The Adventure of the Speckled Band...'"

"...and Jack Stapleton who drowned horribly in the Grimpen Mire in 'The Hound of the Baskervilles...'" I added.

"...not to mention Charles Augustus Milverton—shot to death in cold blood, poor man. It really is an odd thing how many people who displease Sherlock Holmes come to incredibly violent ends."

"Very odd," I agreed, with what I hoped was a pleasant nod in Escoffier's direction. Coupled with Miss Adler's flat, emotionless delivery regarding the deaths of people who crossed Sherlock Holmes, this had the desired effect of wiping the smile off Escoffier's face, who was of a quick enough intelligence to perceive that threatening to expose the living arrangements of Holmes and Miss Adler would not be in his best interests. "I was joking about the kitchen gossip!" he assured Miss Adler with a nervous smile. "Just a little *bon mot*, if you will. I assure you that I am the very soul of discretion—"

"Auguste, you are a complete and utter swine."

"Miss Adler!" Even living in the same household with her had not completely inured me to her forthright way of speaking, but then, she was an American. In England, we certainly think those things, of course, but we rarely say them out loud.

16

"Ask him. He'll tell you himself."

"I am afraid I do not know of what Miss Adler speaks," returned Escoffier. "I am merely a humble chef—"

"—who not too many years ago composed an absolutely wonderful and iconic dessert in which, I believe, peaches played a prominent role. Do you happen to remember the name of it, Auguste?"

While I would never consider myself to be a gourmet in any serious sense of the word, that did ring a bell with me for some reason. "Hang on, I think I've heard of that. It's Peaches Melba, isn't it? Named after Nellie Melba, the opera singer. Do I have that right?"

"Exactly right." Miss Adler stared directly at Escoffier. "Her real name was Helen Porter Mitchell, an Australian soprano who subsequently adopted the name Nellie Melba in honour of her hometown of Melbourne. To celebrate her triumphant performance in Wagner's 'Lohengrin,' Chef Escoffier invented a new dessert featuring peaches poached in syrup, laid on a bed of vanilla ice cream, coated with raspberry purée, sprinkled with rose petals, and veiled with spun sugar..." Miss Adler paused for effect, with Escoffier shrinking beneath her gaze, "...if I recall correctly."

"Yes, that's it!" I agreed, just as another thought struck me. "Quite the coincidence that you happen to be an opera singer too, Miss Adler!"

"Quite." Holmes, who had been uncharacteristically quiet, punctuated this single word by striking a match and lighting his clay pipe.

Escoffier was clearly discomfited by the tenor of this conversation, and in looking around for something with which to change the subject, he caught sight of Miss Adler's birthday breakfast. It was still, I was disappointed to see, completely untouched on the plate as Escoffier picked it up and regarded it with a confused expression.

"Have you a cat, Mr. Holmes?"

"Not that I'm aware."

"Then please allow me..."

And with that, Escoffier strode to the window, opened it, and proceeded to throw Miss Adler's breakfast down to the street below.

"I say!" I objected. "That was Miss Adler's birthday breakfast!"

"Ah, the famous English sense of humour, which I am afraid I will never comprehend. But is it truly your birthday, Irene?"

"Yes," answered Miss Adler.

"Then I shall prepare for you something *magnifique!*"

Escoffier picked up the breakfast tray and headed for the door.

"But Monsieur Escoffier," said Holmes, "you scarcely stopped by to make breakfast. Rather, you appear to have been running from the police."

After his rather dramatic entrance, Escoffier had gradually managed to recover his poise, and he waved away Holmes' words. "A small misunderstanding, it would seem. Not worth discussing while Miss Adler is suffering with an empty stomach." Escoffier turned to her with a gallant smile. "I shall bring you the finest breakfast in the world!"

"But you don't even know what we have in our pantry!" This seemed a sensible enough objection to me, but in response Escoffier simply lifted up his chin and regarded me along the length of his nose.

"I am Escoffier. Your kitchen, Mr. Holmes?"

"This way."

Holmes proceeded to open the door for Escoffier, and a moment later they were gone. I turned to Miss Adler.

"How do you like that? 'I am Escoffier.' Typical French arrogance. Nothing wrong with kippers and kidneys, if you ask me."

If I was hoping for some sort of agreement from Miss Adler, I quickly realised it would not be forthcoming. Indeed, she seemed unduly distracted as she made her way to the sideboard and poured herself a large sherry.

"I say, bit early for a drink. Are you feeling all right, Miss Adler?"

She did not respond immediately. Instead, she took a healthy gulp of sherry, then avoided my gaze as she walked past me towards the window. Standing there looking out at Baker Street, she sipped her sherry and I got the distinct impression that she was gathering herself to say something, so I had the good sense to remain quiet and not badger her.

At length, she began, "May I confess something to you, Doctor? There are times when I wish that I was in love with an idiot. When I wish that my soul mate, the man of my dreams, was a brainless dullard. Unimaginative, incurious, incapable of stringing together anything resembling a series of logical thoughts; in short, a dim, half-witted imbecile. Sadly, I do not have that. My lover is a genius; in fact, genius is too pale and empty a word to even begin to encompass the depth and breadth of his brilliance. Every word is a novel to him, every second a lifetime revealed.

"Emotionally and intellectually, I stand perpetually naked in his presence, every flaw, every blemish, as clear to him as a footprint in new-fallen snow. Make no mistake, I do cherish it.

More than you can ever know. How a single glance between us can communicate an hour's worth of words. How his touch, the slightest pressure of his palm in the small of my back lets me know that he has seen what I have seen, heard what I have heard, and understands what I understand. But at this very moment, I would give a king's ransom to be in love with a complete and utter simpleton."

It was a beautifully composed little speech and quite heartfelt, but I found myself struggling to comprehend precisely what she was driving at, and said as much. "I'm not sure I understand."

Miss Adler turned from the window and came back towards me. "Then let me put it this way—only a woman who has loved a man of genius can appreciate what happiness there is in loving a fool."

Before I had time to try and untangle her meaning, Holmes reentered, and after a glance at both of us, came to a halt. "I'm sorry. I appear to be intruding."

"Not at all," replied Miss Adler. "And we have no secrets between us in these rooms. Tell Dr. Watson what you've already deduced."

"My dear, there's really no need to—"

"Please. If this evolves into a case of some kind, the good Doctor will want details."

"As you wish." Holmes turned towards me, then had the kindness to wait until I had my notebook and pencil in hand. "But surely it's obvious."

"Not to me."

"Quite clearly, Irene and Monsieur Escoffier were lovers. Their time together was brief but intense, and Escoffier was on the verge of naming his most famous dish Peaches Adler, before a rival by the name of Nellie Melba appeared on the scene. Stung and perhaps a tad vengeful, Irene immediately took up with the King of Bohemia, who shortly thereafter brought Miss Adler to our attention in—"

"'A Scandal in Bohemia!' Good Lord." I was scribbling down notes as fast as I could when a thought struck me. "How do you know their relationship was intense?"

"Because I know Irene," returned Holmes.

"And brief?"

"There is no dish named after Miss Adler."

As on numerous other occasions, all of this made perfect sense once Holmes had explained it, and I could now see the events of the past few minutes in a completely new light. When Miss Adler was mingling with the upper echelon of British society as a visiting American contralto, it was only natural that she should have dined at The Savoy Hotel and made the acquaintance of Auguste Escoffier. The fact that he fell in love with her didn't surprise me at all, but it must have been a considerable shock for him to awake in the rooms of Sherlock Holmes to find his supposedly long-dead former lover gazing down at him.

"It was like so many relationships, Doctor," said Miss Adler. "At one time the very centre of the universe, but now nothing more than an embarrassment."

"I'm sorry to hear that."

"Don't be. Monsieur Escoffier was the first link in the chain that brought me here, and I will be forever grateful to him for that."

"As am I," said Holmes.

Woman of the world though she was, all of these revelations had clearly unsettled Miss Adler, and as I thought about it, I began to understand why. Escoffier may well have been the most famous chef in the world when she met him, but he was also a pompous little man, a bit too much in love with himself and his abilities in the kitchen. Yes, perhaps he had made a name for himself with elaborate preparations and sauces to titillate the palates of the upper class, but to put the matter bluntly, he was not Sherlock Holmes.

Seeing Miss Adler's distress, Holmes approached her, laid a hand on her arm, then gently kissed her cheek and said the most romantic thing possible to assure her of his unshakeable love and devotion.

"Now then, more data. What can you tell me about this Escoffier?"

Miss Adler smiled, her eyes shining with gratitude. "Well, he may be a swine, but he is also a genius."

"The two often go hand-in-hand," agreed Holmes.

"His food is revolutionary," continued Miss Adler. "Lighter, fresher, smaller portions, more delicate sauces...he has a staff of eighty at The Savoy and invented a brigade system so that the food is served faster and at the correct temperature. He keeps track of everything each customer orders, can remember every recipe he ever created, and has over sixty recipes for pheasant alone. His best cooking is inspired by women he wants to seduce."

"Married?"

"Of course."

"And The Savoy Hotel," said Holmes. "I know of its reputation, but my interest in mingling with the wealthy and fashionable is confined to when their corpses are still warm."

"It's the most glamourous hotel in the most glamourous city in the world," replied Miss Adler. "Built and owned by Richard

D'Oyly Carte, who made his fortune producing Gilbert and Sullivan's comic operas at The Savoy Theatre in the Strand. He opened The Savoy Hotel next door to his theatre about eight years ago—seven stories, four hundred rooms, electric lights, telephones, elevators, old money mingles with new and it is quite simply *the* place to be seen, because the restaurant is open to the public, not just guests of the hotel. In fact, the hotel and restaurant are merely different versions of the theatre; that is, stages where people dress up and put on a show. Turn almost any corner and you're likely to bump into a duke, a countess, a Rothschild, or a Vanderbilt. Most notably, it enjoys the patronage of the Prince of Wales, who is the very centre of London's social universe."

"It sounds absolutely hideous," remarked Holmes.

"For you, it would be," agreed Miss Adler. "But then, you're a disagreeable curmudgeon with no interest in small talk, the cut of this season's dinner jacket, or who's having an affair with whom. You would much rather be holed up in here with a bloodstain and your chemistry set…which is precisely why I adore you as much as I do."

At that, Holmes took Miss Adler's hand and looked into her eyes. "Watson, I think perhaps Irene and I will take a little walk. Get some fresh air…"

"…perhaps do some investigating regarding all that police activity?" added Miss Adler hopefully.

"My thought precisely."

"But what about Escoffier?" I objected. "He's in our kitchen making breakfast!"

"Then you, my dear Watson, shall be here to sample his creation."

And with that, Holmes and Miss Adler swept towards the door and were gone in an instant.

Chapter Two
An Indecent Proposal

I made my way to the window and watched Holmes and Miss Adler emerge out onto Baker Street, and saw that they were heading in the same direction as the police whistles that had streamed past our door only a few minutes ago. I gave Miss Adler a small wave then stood there for a moment, considering precisely what I should do when Escoffier came back upstairs with Miss Adler's breakfast.

Of course, I knew very well that I shouldn't do anything aside from put it on the table for her to enjoy upon her return, but all the same I was debating as to whether or not I had enough willpower to resist a discreet nibble or two. This was, after all, Auguste Escoffier, the greatest chef in the world, and my rather modest budget didn't allow for regular excursions to the restaurant at The Savoy Hotel.

It was in the midst of these ruminations that I was overcome with the very strong sensation of not being alone in the room. That was absurd, of course. I could quite literally see the steps leading to our front door from where I was standing and hadn't heard anyone coming up the stairs or entering our rooms. Still, I had the overwhelming impression of being watched, and so I turned very slowly, absolutely certain that I would see nothing amiss and no one in the room.

And then, there she was, standing mere feet from me, Marie Chartier, daughter of the late Professor Moriarty, and the woman who had brilliantly exploited the work and tragic life of the Post-Impressionist painter Vincent Van Gogh in the case that I had titled, "The Adventure of the Elusive Ear." In fact, our souvenir of the case, a self-portrait by Van Gogh with a white bandage wrapped around his head, was still on the wall at the insistence of Holmes and Miss Adler. During his short stay with us, Van Gogh had painted it while holed up in my bedroom, and I might add, vandalised my treasured portrait of General "Chinese" Gordon in the process.

But back to Mademoiselle Marie Chartier. While our time together had been of a particularly intense nature, it had also been brief, and I knew very little about Miss Chartier aside from the fact that she was Swiss, spoke with a French accent, and was implacably evil, having decided to style herself as the Napoleoness of Crime in homage to her late father. How she had materialised in our rooms was utterly beyond me, and for the moment she stood absolutely still, a vision of style and loveliness, even with what I perceived to be a fresh duelling scar on her left cheek.

"And so we meet again, Dr. Watson."

It was only the sound of her voice that fully convinced me that she was there in the flesh, and not some kind of phantom or hallucination.

"How the devil did you get in here?"

Miss Chartier offered only an enigmatic smile in return as her eyes wandered around the room. Trying to collect my disordered thoughts as best as I was able, I harkened back to Holmes' dictum, "Whenever you have eliminated the impossible, whatever remains, however improbable, must be the truth." She hadn't come up our stairs or been hiding in the room all along, so clearly she must have somehow gained access to one of our bedroom windows and entered in that manner.

As difficult as it was for me to conceive of a woman clambering up to the second story of a building and then climbing in through a window, past experience had taught me that there were few things beyond the capabilities of Miss Chartier. In any case, the fact that she was standing in front of me was incontestable, and my thoughts immediately ran to what sort of crime she was intent on committing and my own survival.

"I warn you, Miss Chartier, no sudden moves!" I declared in what I hoped was an emphatic fashion, but then instantly realised there was no reason she couldn't do anything she liked. Panicking slightly, I added, "Holmes is in that bedroom right over there! One shout from me and—"

"No. Mr. Holmes is not here. I just saw him leave arm in arm with Miss Adler."

As she continued her examination of the artwork on our walls, I began sidling in what I hoped was a casual fashion towards our sideboard so that I could arm myself. Just as casually, Miss Chartier remarked, "You may go to the sideboard if you wish. Is that where Mr. Holmes keeps his guns?"

"No! I wasn't! I was just—"

"Nonsense. Here, let me help you." With a disturbing air of nonchalance, Miss Chartier moved to the sideboard, opened a drawer, and pulled out a revolver.

"Of course. The Webley British Bulldog..." she paused to open it and spin the cylinder, clearly more familiar with the weapon than most women, or most men for that matter. "*Bien.* Fully loaded."

She looked up at me and my blood ran cold. There was absolutely nothing to stop her from filling me with bullets and then exiting the way she came. But then, our last case involving Miss Chartier had taught me to expect the unexpected from her, and again, she did not disappoint. She closed the cylinder, then approached me and handed me the gun.

"There you are," she said as she raised my arm to point the gun. "Let me just back up a few steps..."

True to her word, she backed away from me, in direct line of fire of the revolver, and then raised her hands.

"...and *voilà!* You have me covered. Do you feel safer now?"

"I feel slightly ridiculous," I replied, which was entirely true. The most dangerous woman in Europe had just magically appeared in our rooms, and to make me feel comfortable, had now armed me with a loaded weapon. I don't know quite what came over me at that point, but the very absurdity of the situation, coupled with a sense of relief that I wasn't writhing on the floor with my blood pumping out of me, prompted me to engage in a little small talk.

"I say, is that a duelling scar on your cheek?" I asked.

Having made her point with the Webley, Miss Chartier plucked it from my hand and proceeded to place it back in the drawer of the sideboard.

"It is nothing. A small disagreement that escalated."

"But you've been wounded!"

"You should see the other fellow...but you'd have to dig down six feet first." It was chilling to hear her talk that way, because having witnessed her skill with a sword during her previous visit, I had no reason to believe that she was telling a tall tale.

She was now strolling about the room, examining various items as they caught her interest, "I see not much has changed since my last visit."

"No. And I don't mean to appear rude, but why are you here? Clearly not to kill Holmes, if you just saw him leaving."

"Wonderfully deduced." She proceeded to pull a sword from among our fireplace tools and pointed it at my chest. "But I could have come here to kill you."

At this, I merely laughed and brushed the sword away, which, to my immense satisfaction, appeared to confuse Miss Chartier.

"Why do you laugh?"

"Because you could have already killed me and because I'm Watson. Good old reliable Watson. Boring, plodding, why is he even in the stories Watson. No one notices me, much less plots my assassination."

As much as I would like to say that I was exaggerating for effect, that was the cold, hard truth of the matter. Whether it was with the police, journalists, or random people in the street, the focus was almost entirely on Sherlock Holmes wherever we went. With his height, hawk-like visage, and erect bearing, he looked every inch the hero that he was. This effect was further exacerbated on cases where we ventured into the countryside and Holmes donned his deerstalker and Inverness cape.

Villagers from miles around would come flocking to the crime scene as news that Sherlock Holmes was in the area spread like wildfire. Holmes, of course, was keenly aware of the effect that he had on people and much of the image that he projected was calculated. He feigned obliviousness, but knew very well that his physical appearance and reputation granted him privileges and access that would be firmly denied to any other member of the general public. As it happens, being regarded as a living legend does have its advantages.

For myself, on the other hand, when I was perceived at all, it was as the harmless drudge trailing in the wake of Sherlock Holmes. Was Holmes an exceptional human being? Of course.

Would he be largely regarded as exceptional were it not for me and my stories in "The Strand Magazine?" Of course not. I had long ago reconciled myself to this state of affairs, but there was still the occasional twinge of jealousy or envy at hearing Holmes lauded to the heavens while my own efforts were dismissed out of hand. Still, as I had just made clear to Miss Chartier, I didn't particularly worry myself about assassination attempts, so there was a certain peace of mind to be had there.

The more pragmatic advantage to my relative anonymity was that no one expected very much of me, and not being the centre of attention has distinct advantages from a writing point of view. Having recovered my equilibrium from Miss Chartier's abrupt appearance and secure in the knowledge that she wasn't here to kill me or anyone else, I concluded that there was no reason I shouldn't play the role of the perfect English gentleman.

"Drink?" I offered, and was gratified to see a small smile flit across her features as she put the sword back amongst the fireplace tools.

"I was hoping you would ask. Sherry."

"Sherry it is."

"Join me, won't you?"

"Why?"

"Please."

I will admit that my mind was racing as I poured two sherries. Had she somehow penetrated our rooms earlier and infused the sherry with some kind of narcotic or other substance? Was she hoping to get me inebriated for some reason? Or, more improbably, given what I assumed was her isolated and peripatetic way of life, was it simply a desire to share a drink with another human being?

"I'm afraid I don't know when Holmes will return, Miss Chartier, but I'm sure he'll welcome a visit from the daughter of Professor Moriarty...especially after your performance the last time you were here with that Van Gogh fellow and Oscar Wilde."

This was a case that had occurred some years previously, which began when a frantic Vincent Van Gogh had showed up at our doorstep begging Holmes to find his missing ear that had been freshly severed. From that quite singular beginning, the case had blossomed into a massive conspiracy concerning the art of Post-Impressionist painters such as Van Gogh, Toulouse-Lautrec, Georges Seurat, and Paul Gauguin, with none other than Marie Chartier orchestrating events to her own considerable advantage.

I had brought Wilde into the case as an expert on all things cultural, and it was his insights into the world of art and the exploitation of artists that had helped Holmes and Miss Adler uncover Miss Chartier's nefarious scheme. Regrettably, but as a mark of her brilliance, she wasn't actually committing any sort of crime in the technical sense of the term, and the case concluded not with her arrest, but in her walking out the door arm in arm with Van Gogh and accompanying him back to the French town of Arles. Van Gogh, poor man, was utterly infatuated with Miss Chartier, and not two years later we heard of his unfortunate suicide, although Holmes hinted to me very strongly that he doubted that Van Gogh had taken his own life.

As I handed Miss Chartier her glass of sherry, she remarked, "A most interesting case, *n'est-ce pas?* I am so glad you took my advice and did not write up the story for 'The Strand Magazine.'"

"No need to be coy, Miss Chartier," I returned. "You know very well why I couldn't publish it. Your threat to expose the relationship between Holmes and Miss Adler accomplished that task very nicely. Nevertheless, I did write the story and then put it safely away...for future generations."

"Really? And what did you call it?"

"The Adventure of the Elusive Ear."

"I like that...to 'The Adventure of the Elusive Ear.'"

She raised her glass and we toasted one another, then sipped our sherries. It was all quite proper and civilised, and I wondered just how long this façade would last, but determined to enjoy it while it did.

"It was a pretty little case, was it not?" continued Miss Chartier. "It deserves to be set down for posterity, and I must confess, I do wish that I could read it. You have a most wonderful way with words."

"Seriously? You really think so?"

"I do. The right word at the right moment...is there anything more beautiful and seductive?"

Well aware that I was being steered into darker waters, I looked up at Van Gogh's self-portrait, interested to hear what she might have to say about her relationship with him.

"Damned shame about Van Gogh. We all read about his unfortunate death."

"Yes, poor Vincent."

"When he was here with you in our rooms, he had yet to sell a single painting. But since his suicide, I understand his work is becoming more and more popular. Do you agree that it was suicide, Miss Chartier? There are rumours that he was murdered."

"Vincent was a troubled soul," demurred Miss Chartier. "I suspect he was looking for the peace that he could not find on earth."

"How fortunate for you that he gave you most of the art that he created in Arles."

"Indeed," Miss Chartier sipped her sherry thoughtfully. "Human nature is a curious thing, is it not? It is almost as if we want our writers and artists to destroy themselves for our entertainment. Somehow, their self-destruction becomes romanticised and serves as proof of their suffering and sincerity. That would be my advice to any struggling artist—suffer and die—and the sooner the better."

"In other words," I added, "your plan to exploit the miserable lives of the Post-Impressionists for your own profit would appear to be coming along quite nicely."

"Oh, yes. I should say so. Do you despise me for it?"

The directness of her answer unsettled me slightly, but I should have expected no less.

"That's a bit harsh," I began. "I always like to give people the benefit of the doubt…see the world as they see it, you might say. Who knows what circumstances or events lead people to do the things they do? If I think about your life, for example, you had a rough start of it obviously, your father being the Napoleon of Crime and all…I suspect you had a difficult childhood."

"Which means?"

"Well, perhaps with a different upbringing, different environment, your life might have gone in another direction entirely, rather than attempting to become the Napoleoness of Crime, if you will."

"Or perhaps darkness and villainy run in my blood." Flashing her green eyes at me, her lips curled into a small smile. "Another sherry, I think."

I looked down and was surprised to see that my sherry glass was empty as Miss Chartier took it from my hand and headed to the sideboard. I watched her closely, trying to put myself into Holmes' shoes and imagining what he would observe and deduce, but it was hopeless. As she came back towards me with two glasses of sherry, I decided that my only course of action was to be as direct as possible.

"What are you up to, Miss Chartier?"

"*Moi?*"

"You're not fooling me. Much as I would like to believe that this is purely a social call and that you're desperate for my fascinating company, I know very well that you have some sort of plot or scheme in mind."

"Indeed. You see right through me, Doctor, so I may as well confess that I came here with a three-part plan. First, I wanted to get you alone..."

Miss Chartier raised her glass and I reflexively raised mine as well as we toasted one another again.

"Second, I wanted to get a glass or two of sherry into you to ease your nerves..."

"And third?" I returned, mentally resolving that this would be my last sherry of the day.

"I need you."

"Come now, Miss Chartier," I remonstrated. "What you mean is that you need Holmes. I know you intend to flatter me, but there's no point in pretending otherwise."

"You believe that I am pretending?"

"Well, of course you are. Trust me, the line of people who have tried to use me to get to Holmes would stretch from here to Cambridge. Quite frankly, I must confess myself a little disappointed in your lack of ingenuity and enterprise."

"Oh, Dr. Watson..." she began with a rueful smile. "Dear, dear Dr. Watson. I can only imagine the amount of disrespect that you suffer in silence on a regular basis. And I am sorry to see that it has come to the point where you now even disrespect yourself. But I assure you that I am here to see you, and you alone. You see, Mr. Holmes has Miss Adler. They have one another. Whom do you have? Whom do I have? No one. That is why we need each other."

These were dangerous waters indeed. I could practically feel my feet being lifted from the seabed and the tide of Miss Chartier's personality pulling me out into the depths. Still, I couldn't help but be intrigued by the direction in which our conversation was headed.

"In what way, exactly?" I enquired.

"It is quite simple. For all of his talents, there is one area in which the great Sherlock Holmes cannot hold a candle to Dr. Watson."

"Nonsense."

"You are too modest."

"Very well then, I'll play along. What area might that be?"

"Storytelling. I want you to help me tell a story."

With the way she said it and the way she looked at me, I had no doubt whatsoever that she was telling the truth. Similarly, the way she said it and looked at me made the hairs on the back of my neck stand up. I could almost see the pit of quicksand forming at my feet, and yet, it occurred to me that perhaps I could avoid whatever infamous or tragic fate Miss Chartier had planned for my future. After all, storytelling was my world, not hers. Then again, painting had been Van Gogh's world, and he had wound up with a bullet in his stomach. Still, I hadn't committed to anything, and getting a little more information couldn't hurt.

"A story about what?" I asked.

"What happens in London tomorrow?"

The oddness of the question took me aback for a moment, but I knew instantly to what she was referring.

"Why, it's Queen Victoria's Diamond Jubilee, of course! She's been on the throne sixty years now, so tomorrow has been declared a National Holiday." I turned my gaze to the portrait of Queen Victoria on our wall. "Remarkable woman. Tiny little thing, but during her reign England has become the richest and most powerful country in the world."

"Yes," agreed Miss Chartier, "and it is the 'richest' part that I like best. However, I have a problem. I am not English, and the British nobility are a very close-knit group. Everyone knows everyone. So, how would I penetrate that society? How could I gain the trust, for example, of Queen Victoria's son, the Prince of Wales?"

At this, I could feel myself relax. Whatever improbable scheme Miss Chartier had in mind was nothing more than a fantasy, because the royal family, with their various guards and attendants, would never allow a common foreigner like Miss Chartier near the Prince of Wales, aside perhaps from a brief dalliance, the nature of which doesn't bear going into any further. Feeling a touch charitable due to the sherry, I thought it would be best to be candid with her so she would see that she was wasting her time.

"Well, you can't. It's that simple. It's impossible."

"Perhaps for Marie Chartier, but not for...the Duchess of Killarney!"

It would be impossible to describe the effect that those last four words had on me, because they were delivered with a perfect Irish accent. And before I had a chance to say anything, Miss Chartier then proceeded to execute a few steps from an Irish jig, then looked at me with the most angelic smile I have ever seen on a human being's face.

"Oh, faith and begorrah, I've given poor Dr. Watson a wee shock, I'm afraid."

It was absolutely uncanny. Mere seconds ago I had been in the presence of an evil Swiss temptress, but now I was looking at a pure and simple Irish lass of noble blood, her eyes shining at me with all the innocence of child.

"Your accent..." I finally managed. "That's absolutely wonderful! It's as if you were born in Ireland!"

Presumably for my benefit, she kept up her impersonation. "Do you really think so? You wouldn't just be flattering a poor Irish lass now, would you?"

"Not at all! No, it's astonishing..."

Momentarily disoriented, I did what I often do in such situations; that is, I reached for my notebook, but then stopped. What could I possibly write down? "Miss Chartier can speak with an Irish accent and dance an Irish jig?" It was ludicrous.

Observing my confusion, Miss Chartier laughed and continued on in her new guise as the Duchess of Killarney.

"Oh, go on now, get your wee notebook out. I know you want to, and you're going to need it."

"Well, perhaps I'll just jot down a point or two..." I agreed, but having no real notion of what I could possibly write as Miss Chartier guided me to the divan.

"There we are. You sit down like a good lad, and I will explain everything to you. It's really quite simple. The beautiful and recently widowed Duchess of Killarney happens to be staying at The Savoy Hotel at the moment, where last week she had a wee bit o' the luck o' the Irish, and who do you think she met? The Prince of Wales himself."

"Hang on...The Savoy Hotel? That's where Auguste Escoffier is the head chef."

"So he is. And just between us, both Monsieur Escoffier and the Prince of Wales find the Duchess of Killarney absolutely fascinating."

Still scrambling to somehow orient myself to this new universe that Miss Chartier had created out of nothing, I retained enough of my wits to understand the full import of what she was saying. "Oh my God. They're both in love with you."

"It is what I do." I was indescribably grateful that Miss Chartier had reverted back to her natural French accent. The world stopped spinning and it was somehow perversely comforting to once again find myself in the presence of a woman I knew to be a master criminal.

"Unfortunately," Miss Chartier continued, "there are some people around the Prince who do not like the Duchess of Killarney very much. They feel she is a woman of doubtful reputation and uncertain revenue."

"But it's a brilliant character!" I replied, with perhaps a touch too much enthusiasm. "First of all, she is apparently of noble blood, which will make the Prince of Wales feel she is of his class. But then, she's Irish, so she's just different enough to separate herself from everyone else he knows!"

"I knew you would understand."

"But still," I went on, "you're faced with one major problem; namely, this Duchess of Killarney doesn't really exist!"

"A small detail. The Prince of Wales wants her to exist. He is one of those sad people for whom the truth is much less important than what he wishes the truth to be. Nevertheless, it occurred to me that I could use someone to vouch for me. And who do I know who is more decent, more upstanding, and more English than Dr. John Watson?"

With that, things began to come into sharper focus, although what the final picture might be, I wasn't sure I wanted to know. And so, like a rider aboard a runaway horse approaching a cliff, I determined to jump off while I still could.

"Now see here, Miss Chartier, I don't know what you're trying to get me involved in, but the answer is no."

"But you have not heard what I am willing to offer you."

"The answer is still no. I cannot be bought. Not with money, not with a Van Gogh original, not with anything."

I said all this as emphatically as I could, with the intention that Miss Chartier should pack up whatever scheme she had in mind and be on her way. I had seen the abyss opening up at my feet and was rather proud of the fact that through sheer willpower I had managed to step back. However, Miss Chartier was not done with me.

"But I know your weak spot," she asserted.

"You do?"

And as Miss Chartier arched one perfect eyebrow, I was suddenly thrown back in time to the case of Van Gogh's missing ear, when at a crucial point in our investigation she had taken me by the lapels and forcibly bestowed upon me a lengthy kiss. There was nothing remotely romantic or affectionate about it, she was simply proving a point, and prove it she did, to the extent that there are still nights when I am drifting off to sleep that I can feel the warmth of her breath and smell her sandalwood perfume. Given that experience, I was much wiser now, and felt well prepared to fend her off, if need be.

"If you are suggesting that you could somehow use your womanly wiles to seduce me into a compromising position, I assure you that—"

"If I wanted to seduce you, you would be on your knees right now." The certainty with which Miss Chartier uttered those words was more than a little unnerving, as if she had blandly observed that the earth orbits the sun, and so it was with no little sense of relief that I realised she hadn't finished her train of thought.

"No, Dr. Watson. I am not offering you money, or art, or the single most shattering sexual experience of your lifetime. I am offering you something much, much better. You help me tell my story and I will return the favour, by giving you the greatest Sherlock Holmes story ever."

Two sherries or not, she now had my full and undivided attention.

"Oh really? How so?"

"Think of it..." she began to spin her web before my very eyes. "The daughter of Professor Moriarty...the Prince of Wales...The Savoy Hotel...power, wealth, desire...the English Monarchy, oh, and that is only the tip of the iceberg. You are an Escoffier with words, Dr. Watson. What a feast you could create with those ingredients."

"There are certain elements of interest, I suppose..." I replied, even as I ticked off all of these quite incredible plot points in my mind and hoped that Miss Chartier wouldn't be able to read my interest. However, I knew it was a losing game as Miss Chartier came to the divan and sat quite close to me, her eyes searching mine.

"Come now, Doctor. It is just us two. Alone. No one else needs to know. It will be our little secret...so look at me, and tell me what you see."

So, this was it. Since the moment I had turned and seen her in our rooms, my mind had been oscillating between self-preservation as a human being and self-interest as a writer. Once it became abundantly clear that she had no form of violence in mind, my thoughts instinctively ran to where they almost always go. I knew very well what I saw when I looked at her, and so did she. Any form of denial or subterfuge would be pointless, so I determined to lay my cards on the table and see where things went from there.

"Material," I began. "Damn it all, absolutely amazing material! You're beautiful, you're brilliant, and you are a demonic temptress completely and utterly steeped in evil. It's beyond wonderful!"

"Quite so," Miss Chartier patted my hand, and I suppose we were both glad to have all of the posturing behind us. "And the Diamond Jubilee...the *Diamond* Jubilee...that is most suggestive, don't you think? And that is why I am here. I am not quite sure how events will unfold just yet, but for the moment I need a storyteller, my very own *fabricateur*...I need you, Dr. Watson. And you need me."

"What—I can't believe I'm saying this, but what, exactly, are you asking me to do?"

"My request is a modest one. Should we, by chance, see one another in the next day or two, you simply address me as your old friend, the Duchess of Killarney. In other words, do what you do best. Tell a story."

Before I could ask her to elaborate on what kind of story she had in mind, I heard footsteps on the stairs and Escoffier singing "La Marseillaise" at considerable volume. In truth, I had completely forgotten that the greatest chef in the world was making breakfast in our kitchen, for that was the effect of Miss Chartier's mesmerising presence. For her part, Miss Chartier didn't seem alarmed at all at having our private *tête-à-tête* interrupted. Instead, handing me her sherry glass, she smiled and then disappeared into Holmes' bedroom just as Escoffier entered, bearing a platter and marching as if he were in the Bastille Day parade.

Chapter Three

Our Masked Visitor

As it turned out, for all of his talents, the greatest chef in the world couldn't carry a tune, but what he lacked in talent and technique, he made up for with pure patriotic enthusiasm, the walls fairly ringing as he marched to the centre of the room, bellowing the French national anthem at the top of his lungs.

"Allons enfants de la Patrie,
Le jour de gloire est arrivé!
Aux armes, citoyens,
Formez vos bataillons,
Marchons, marchons!
Qu'un sang impur
Abreuve nos sillons!"

Having mercifully finished, Escoffier looked around the room in bewilderment. "What is this? Where are Miss Adler and Mr. Holmes?"

"Who?" Discombobulated by the two sherry glasses I was holding and the disappearance of Miss Chartier, I was trying to determine whether or not she had, indeed, fled the premises. Looking around for a place to put the glasses, I finally settled on the sideboard before turning my attention to Escoffier and attempting to answer his question. "Oh, you mean Holmes and Miss Adler! Well, they've…what have they done...they've gone out...in the street...to go someplace...that's outside...where the street is..."

"But I have prepared breakfast for Miss Adler! *Voilà!*"

Escoffier removed the cloche from the plate, uncovering what looked suspiciously like scrambled eggs to my untutored eye, with a white birthday candle in the centre of the fluffy yellow mass.

"What is it?"

"Scrambled eggs!"

"Ha!" I couldn't help but laugh. "Scrambled eggs? So this is the gourmet creation of the greatest chef in the world?"

Instead of answering, Escoffier took a fork, heaped it with scrambled eggs, then directed it towards my mouth. With no desire to have my lips pierced by the tines of the fork, I opened my mouth and a moment later was experiencing one of the most exquisite things I have ever tasted in my life. Looking again at the plate, it certainly seemed to be nothing more than a pile of scrambled eggs, but once in my mouth, it became so much more than that.

"This can't be just..." I began. "What's in this?"

Again, Escoffier regarded me along the length of his considerable nose, "Merely eggs stirred quickly over low heat with a clove of garlic on the end of a fork. *Surtout, faites simple.* That is my motto, Dr. Watson. Above all, keep it simple."

"And where in God's name did you find a birthday candle? I practically tore apart the kitchen looking for one."

"I didn't find it. I made it. Out of sugar. See for yourself."

Scraping my fingernail across the candle, I put it to my lips and was stunned to taste nothing more than pure sugar. While I may not have fully appreciated Escoffier's talent when he first appeared in our rooms hysterically waving a cleaver, I certainly appreciated them now. For all of his posturing and histrionics, he was unquestionably a wizard in the kitchen.

"That's absolutely remarkable," I exclaimed. "Astounding!"

Escoffier waved away my praise, no doubt hearing the same thing every day at The Savoy Hotel. "I am Escoffier. I can create any dish in any shape or form you desire, for the finest food must engage all of the senses...the sizzle of a steak, the snap of a pea. Every menu should be a poem of anticipation and every meal should be a symphony for the senses, but do you know the most important ingredient in all of my dishes?"

Having no earthly clue what his secret ingredient might be, I shook my head, and even though we were the only two people in the room, Escoffier put his lips to my ear and whispered, "It is love, *mon ami*. It is love."

Nodding in understanding, I picked up the fork to have some more scrambled eggs, but Escoffier slammed the cloche back on top of the plate.

"*Non, non, non!* This is for Miss Adler..." Escoffier then reached into his jacket, pulled out a letter-sized envelope, and handed it to me. "...and this is for Mr. Holmes—the reason I came here in the first place. I have enemies, Doctor! Invisible enemies! Will you please use your influence with Mr. Holmes on my behalf?"

"Perhaps," I replied, recognising an opportunity to get a better grasp of the great chef's character and the kind of man we were dealing with. "Would you be willing to answer three questions first?"

"Anything!"

"Miss Adler claims that you can remember every dish you ever created and that you have over sixty recipes for pheasant alone. Surely that's an exaggeration, yes?"

"Make your way to The Savoy, Dr. Watson, and I shall personally prepare a pheasant for you. What is your pleasure? *Faison à la mode d'Alcantra*, stuffed with duck foie gras and quartered truffles, marinated for three days in port wine, then cooked *en casserole* with more truffles; *Faison à l'Angoumoise*, stuffed with pork fat, truffles, chestnuts, wrapped in bacon, then roasted and served with a truffled Périgueux sauce—"

I held up my hand. "You have made your point, Monsieur Escoffier. Thank you. My second question involves a friend of mine, Oscar Wilde, who was a frequent visitor to The Savoy Hotel and dined there frequently. May I assume that you made his acquaintance?"

I let the question hang as I observed Escoffier's face fall. "Mr. Wilde was a wonderful man. *Is* a wonderful man, I should say. It was my pleasure to serve him anything he desired, for I have never met anyone so witty, charming, and kind."

"Indeed he is," I concurred. "And yet he was arrested and sentenced to prison two years ago for crimes he allegedly committed at The Savoy Hotel."

"A terrible incident. I am sorry to say that The Savoy failed him. A hotel has many secrets, Dr. Watson, and the fact that we failed to help Mr. Wilde keep his private life private is one of the greatest regrets of my life."

I nodded, having heard what I wanted to hear, and slipped Escoffier's envelope into my pocket. "I'll see to it that Mr. Holmes gives your case his closest attention."

"Thank you!" Relief washed over Escoffier's face. "I am most grateful! And now I must get back to The Savoy. But I shall return!"

Escoffier quickly made his way to the door, but then stopped and turned. "Ah, but I believe you said that you had three questions?"

"Yes, but I'm afraid the last one is a trifle indiscreet. On second thought, perhaps I shouldn't—"

"Not at all, Dr. Watson! Please, what is it you wish to know?"

"Were you really romantically involved with both Miss Adler and Nellie Melba at the same time?"

Escoffier offered a small smile and a shrug. "What can I say? Mistresses are like desserts. They are both bad for you, but if you are going to have one, you might as well have two."

With that, Escoffier was gone, and as I reached for my notebook to jot down his pithy parting words, I was alarmed to hear a bedroom door open. Turning, I observed Miss Chartier emerging from Holmes' bedroom holding a black negligee.

"*Ooh la la!* Miss Adler, she has a nice taste in clothes..." Pirouetting with the negligee about the room, I will readily admit to a twinge of regret that she wasn't actually wearing it, but a moment later I am happy to say that my sensible British upbringing reasserted itself.

"Really, Miss Chartier! Put that back this instant!"

Draping the negligee over the divan, Miss Chartier made her way to the breakfast table, where she had observed the plate left by Escoffier.

"And what have we here? Breakfast from Chef Escoffier?"

As she lifted the cloche to reveal the scrambled eggs, I realised with a jolt that I had an imminent disaster on my hands. In a moment, Miss Chartier would be finishing off the scrambled eggs and I would be left with an empty plate to explain to Holmes and Miss Adler when they returned. I couldn't very well say that I had eaten them, because that would be the height of rudeness. Then again, I couldn't simply wash the plate and put it away, because Escoffier had promised to make Miss Adler breakfast. As half a dozen possible explanations flashed through my brain, each more unlikely than the last, Miss Chartier sniffed at the eggs, and then to my indescribable relief, turned up her nose and put the cloche back on the plate.

"Pah! Typical. Everything is garlic and truffles and foie gras with Escoffier. It is too much. I am a simple girl at heart." Turning to me, she put on her most winning smile. "Now then, as to our little arrangement...will you tell a story for me?"

"And at what cost to perfectly innocent people? Who will get hurt?"

"No one. It is merely a little charade I want to play, although it is possible I may profit slightly from the game, but from people who will never notice the loss, and a man who is far from innocent."

"Are you slandering the good name of the Prince of Wales?" Yes, I am afraid that knee-jerk patriotism can cause people to do and say completely idiotic things, and that's a tendency from which I have never been entirely immune, although I like to think I have learned a sobering lesson or two on the subject over the years. In this particular case, I hadn't learned anything yet, but Miss Chartier was making arrangements to remedy that sooner than I imagined.

"Clearly, you do not know His Royal Highness," she remarked, "but that will change quite soon. I am moving my pieces into position, Dr. Watson. If I might be presumptuous enough to quote the great Sherlock Holmes, 'The game is afoot.' The only question for you is, will you be a pawn, yet again? Or are you ready to play the role of the knight?"

I had to give her credit. Even without a sword in her hand, she was capable of inflicting a thousand tiny cuts, and her chess metaphor was quite apt. I could see that her opening moves had involved making the acquaintance of both the Prince of Wales and Escoffier at The Savoy Hotel in the guise of the widowed

Duchess of Killarney. With both men falling under her spell, she then made her way to 221B Baker Street, being perhaps the only person in history intent on speaking not to Sherlock Holmes, but to me. This in itself was flattering enough, but then she had set before me an almost irresistible bait; that is, the prospect of being a part of the greatest Sherlock Holmes story ever. Now, to put me fully under her spell, she had quite cleverly played upon my feelings of inadequacy and resentment at being perpetually in the shadow of Sherlock Holmes.

Even as I was well aware of what she was doing and that I should show her the door before she could lure me in any further with her siren song, more than anything I desperately wanted to know what would happen next, which was precisely what she was counting on. As I considered how I might best respond to her proposal without actually aiding and abetting what was no doubt intended to be an incredible and audacious crime, all of those thoughts were dashed from my head at the sound of the downstairs door opening and then footsteps ascending the stairs.

"Good God! It's Holmes and Irene! They mustn't find you here!"

Just as with Escoffier's entrance, Miss Chartier didn't seem alarmed in the least, merely moving to pick up the black negligee. "Do not worry, *mon chéri*. Whenever I enter a room, I always have two exits..." Draping the negligee over my chest, she once again put on her Irish accent. "...and the Duchess of Killarney will be back in two shakes of a lamb's tail!"

With impeccable timing, she disappeared into Holmes' bedroom just as the door opened and Holmes and Miss Adler appeared, looking quite refreshed after their stroll around the neighbourhood. Straining to hear any noises Miss Chartier might be making during her escape, it was clearly apparent to Holmes that I was somewhat distracted.

"Watson?"

"Oh, hello." Was that a window I heard opening?

"What are you doing?"

"Standing here. As one does." And was that the window closing?

I then became aware that Miss Adler was looking at me oddly. "Are you wearing one of my negligees?"

Looking down, I could see that I did, in fact, appear to be wearing the negligee, as it was draped over my chest and hanging down to my feet. It was clearly an awkward situation, and in the heat of the moment I'm afraid that I panicked a little. Not wanting to reveal the exchange that had just taken place between Miss Chartier and myself, I finally managed to say, "I can explain...well, this is a little embarrassing, but you see, the thing of it is, sometimes if I'm writing a story and I get a bit stuck finding the voice of this or that character, I find it useful to dress in the manner of that character. So, king, beggar, old, young, man, woman..."

Picking up the thread, Miss Adler added, "So when you're writing a female character, you wear my clothes?"

"Not all the time! Not often, really. Hardly ever, as a matter of fact...just when I have a bit of writer's block. Awfully sorry. I should have asked."

Desperately seeking to change the subject, I draped the negligee over the divan and pointed to the plate that Escoffier had brought in. "That's food...for you, Miss Adler. Escoffier made some eggles scram...scrambled eggs!"

In retrospect, of course, I can see how foolishly I was behaving, but I had been more than a little rattled by Miss

Chartier's visit and was still struggling to get my wits about me. Had I agreed to help her in whatever nefarious scheme she had planned? I wasn't entirely sure.

"And what of Monsieur Escoffier?" asked Holmes.

"Gone!" I replied. "Somewhere. No idea. It's a big city, London. Could be anywhere..."

"Well," continued Holmes, "apparently his arrival here just ahead of the police was, in fact, completely coincidental. They were responding to a robbery further down the street, but his guilty conscience seems to have got the better of him."

"Yes! That's why he was coming here, Holmes! He said he had invisible enemies and left this letter for you!"

Pulling the envelope from my pocket, I gave it to Holmes and at once Miss Adler was by his side as he removed the letter and they both examined it closely.

"Let's see what we have here...industrial paper..." began Holmes.

"...a broad-nibbed pen..." added Miss Adler.

"...coarse, simple strokes..."

"...which indicates the writer is trying to obscure his or her identity..."

I knew that Holmes and Miss Adler could go on in this vein for several minutes—speculating what country in Europe the paper was from, whether the writer was left-handed, which London stores sold this particular brand of ink, and so on. However, at last having had a moment or two to consider the overall situation with all of its implications, I realised that it would be best if I simply told them about the visit of Marie Chartier. In the first place, I doubted that my story about wearing Miss Adler's negligee had fooled them for a moment, and no doubt there were any number of other clues that I had failed to take into account, and so I decided to make a clean breast of it.

"I say Holmes, there is something else you should know..." I began, but Holmes and Miss Adler were like two bulldogs with a bone as they continued to examine the letter.

"It appears to be a list of various crimes and indiscretions..."

"...being committed by Auguste Escoffier at The Savoy Hotel..."

Persistent if nothing else, I made another attempt to get their attention, "We just had a rather special visitor..."

"...so it seems to be an effort at some form of extortion or blackmail..." continued Holmes as if I weren't even in the room.

"...but with no demands and no signature..." added Miss Adler.

"...simply the final words, 'From One Who Knows.'"

Feeling that now was my chance, I made yet another attempt, "Holmes, I really must tell you—"

Holmes whirled on me, irritated to have had his train of thought broken, "Watson, please! A little silence. Irene and I are working!"

Holmes held the letter up to the light, anxious to wring every last bit of information from it. "So, it's a warning of some kind..."

"...apparently from someone very intimate with The Savoy Hotel..." added Miss Adler.

"...although whether an employee or guest is difficult to say. You know the man, Irene. Are these accusations consistent with Chef Escoffier's personality?"

"Sadly, yes. He is a man of incredible talent, and like many such men, feels that the rules should not apply to him. The same may be said for his close friend and the director of The Savoy Hotel, a man by the name of César Ritz."

"Holmes," I interjected, "if you could please listen to me, it's about—"

"Ritz..." Holmes raised one finger, asking for silence, "...Ritz. I recognise the name."

With that, I gave up, sat down and brought out my notebook, on the off chance that this tangent into the exciting world of hotel managers had anything to do with the case.

"You should," said Miss Adler. "César Ritz is the most celebrated hotel manager in all of Europe. Up to now merely an employee, but apparently with plans to open his own luxury hotel in Paris, with none other than Auguste Escoffier as the head chef."

"That's most suggestive," said Holmes. "Does this Ritz come from money?"

"Far from it. I believe he began life as a Swiss peasant— herding goats and sheep, but he has much greater ambitions for himself. I do know that prior to coming to London, he and Escoffier worked together at the Grand Hôtel National in Lucerne..."

"Ah!" exclaimed Holmes. "Now things begin to come into sharper focus. Consider that the essence of this case so far is that we have two extraordinarily talented and ambitious gentlemen with Swiss connections, both currently employed at The Savoy Hotel, who are in need of large sums of money to open their own luxury hotel in Paris, and who are possibly involved in a criminal enterprise to bring that eventuality about, which obviously brings to mind—"

"—Marie Chartier!" I fairly shouted.

"Excellent, Watson! Yes indeed, Marie Chartier, who is also from Switzerland and is no doubt familiar with both Escoffier and Ritz, by reputation at the very least, and quite possibly on more intimate terms if there is criminal activity associated with The Savoy Hotel."

"You think she's involved in this?" asked Miss Adler.

"No idea," replied Holmes. "But whenever I begin to perceive a dark web being woven, my mind instinctively turns to the formidable Miss Chartier."

Miss Adler appeared to take umbrage at this remark and lifted Holmes' chin with her forefinger. "I thought I was the only formidable woman you knew."

"You don't mind a little competition, do you?"

"Not at all."

I knew what was coming next and was not disappointed, as Holmes and Miss Adler fell into a passionate embrace more suitable for midnight in a French bordello than the middle of the day in an English flat. The prospect of a new and potentially exciting case invariably stirred what I'll delicately refer to as primal feelings between them, so I put my notebook away and picked up a newspaper, keenly aware that their interest had veered from the case and it might be some time before it returned to matters at hand. At length, Holmes disengaged himself long enough from Miss Adler to ask, "Oh Watson, was there something you wanted to say?"

Feeling a bit peevish by this point, I replied, "No, nothing. You two are doing wonderfully. You don't need my help, I can see that. Just throw good old Watson a few crumbs after the case is over. That's all I need."

"Now, now, there's no need to get all sullen and mopey," Holmes chided. "There was something you wanted to tell us. What is it?"

Clearly, I now had ample opportunity to inform Holmes and Miss Adler of Miss Chartier's remarkable appearance and her plans to perpetrate some kind of outlandish crime involving Chef Escoffier and the Prince of Wales. But yes, my feelings had been a bit ruffled by being so peremptorily dismissed by Holmes, and added to that was Miss Chartier's goading use of the word "pawn" to describe my contributions to our cases. There was no immediate crisis that I could see, and so I determined that it would do Holmes and Miss Adler a bit of good to realise that when I spoke it might serve them well in the future if they actually listened to me.

"Nothing of importance," I said to Holmes. "I simply wanted to inform you that Chef Escoffier said he would be back."

Both Holmes and Miss Adler appeared to accept this as reasonable enough, and Miss Adler was now eyeing the breakfast tray and moving towards it with serious intent. "I was really hoping Auguste would make me one of his famous soufflés, but I'll nibble on this as I freshen up."

Picking up the tray, she headed for her bedroom as I called after her, "Take it from me, I had a small bite, and it's absolutely wonderful! Even the candle is delicious, for God's sake!"

As she closed the door behind her, I returned my attention to my newspaper and an article full of details on tomorrow's Diamond Jubilee activities, only to realise that Holmes was staring at me. This, I had learned over the years, was almost never a good thing. It usually meant that he knew something and was wondering if I knew the same thing but had somehow neglected to tell him, which in this case was entirely accurate.

Still, I determined to make him play his hand, and so I focused on the article in front of me, which described the Queen's six-mile parade route from Buckingham Palace to St Paul's Cathedral, and added the interesting detail that complimentary beer and pipe tobacco would be available to the crowds courtesy of tea magnate Sir Thomas Lipton.

"I say, Watson...everything all right?"

"Hmm?" I looked up from the paper, shaping my features into what I hoped was the expression of a perfectly innocent child. "Oh, yes! Fine. Splendid. Lovely morning!"

I hadn't returned my attention to the paper for more than five seconds before I became aware that Holmes was pointing to the two empty sherry glasses on the sideboard.

"Curious. Two empty sherry glasses. Those weren't there when Irene and I left."

If the old boy was expecting a full confession, he wasn't going to get it from me, at least not yet. Instead, taking inspiration from Miss Chartier's kind words regarding my storytelling abilities, I decided to spin a tale out of thin air.

"Oh, the sherry glasses...yes. When Escoffier brought in the plate of scrambled eggs I remarked that they would go well with some toast, and Escoffier apparently thought I was proposing a toast to the eggs. Lost in translation, don't you know. I didn't want to make him feel awkward, so I poured some sherry and we drank a toast...to his eggs."

It was a ridiculous tale, of course, but I did have the satisfaction of seeing Holmes nonplussed for a moment just as our bell rang. Folding my paper and setting it down, I went to the window, well aware that Holmes was watching me closely. Looking down on Baker Street, I observed that a hansom cab was parked in front of our door.

"It would appear we have a client!"

In an instant, Miss Adler emerged from her bedroom and she and Holmes moved to the window together.

"Interesting…" began Miss Adler, "…a private hansom cab with no markings..."

"...and the windows blacked out as well to shield the passenger from prying eyes," added Holmes. "Most intriguing. Watson, would you mind—"

"Yes, yes! Of course!" I was already halfway to the door, anxious to see what sort of visitor this mystery person would turn out to be. Making it down our seventeen steps in good time, upon opening our front door I was stunned to see, for only the second time in my life, a man wearing a mask out in public. The first occurrence had been in "A Scandal in Bohemia," when the King of Bohemia had attempted to appear in our rooms incognito.

Holmes, of course, had seen through his disguise immediately, and shortly thereafter largely lost interest in the King's troubles once he had met Irene Adler, who at that particular point in time was blackmailing the King due to the fact that he was, as she forthrightly put it, "a complete bastard."

In this instance I found myself face-to-face with a rather stout fellow wearing a black mask, gloves, and carrying a silver-topped cane, with a feather-festooned hat beneath his arm. Most extraordinarily, he appeared to be wearing the uniform of a British Field Marshal, with medals strewn like confetti all over his chest. In my military experience, I had found that there were some men that a uniform quite suited. Invariably, these were modest, soft-spoken men whose every order was followed instantly, and would have been followed instantly even if they had been wearing rags. Somehow, their carriage and demeanour communicated a natural confidence and authority, regardless of rank. Far away from the froth and frippery of the dress parade, those were the men habitually looked up to by every man in a regiment.

On the other hand, there were men of an entirely different calibre—weak, ignorant, and fearful, who imagined that a uniform somehow transformed them into the kind of men they hoped to be. Realising that they would never be well regarded for their courage or intellect, they relied on their uniform to somehow garner them the respect that would otherwise elude them entirely. Looking our visitor up and down as he stood there with his chest puffed out and staring down his nose at me, I got the distinct impression that I was gazing upon a man whose most fervent hope was that I wouldn't look any deeper than the shiny brass buttons adorning his jacket.

Still, a client is a client, and if he could dress up like this and afford a private hansom cab, then there was a good chance there was money to be made. Bearing that in mind, I bowed slightly and then escorted him up the stairs. Due to his bulk, this was by no means a rapid process, but at length we reached the top of the stairs and I held the door open for him as he entered our rooms.

Without so much as a glance back at me, he handed me his hat and strode to the centre of the room, striking a pose that I'm sure he hoped looked casually elegant, and gazed vaguely upward at nothing in particular. Holmes and Miss Adler glanced at one another, no doubt as curious as I was to see what this exotic creature would have to say, and we didn't have to wait long.

"Mr. Holmes, I presume?"

Holmes nodded, perhaps not trusting himself to speak.

"I am the Duke of Lancaster. I come to you for help in the most dire circumstances imaginable, but would first like to ascertain that you really do possess the powers attributed to you. So then, based upon my appearance, what can you tell me?"

This, I knew from experience, was not the best opening with Holmes, who loathed pretence and pomposity more than any man alive, and Holmes did not disappoint.

"I can tell you that you are a middle-aged man who enjoys eating. Thank you so much for stopping by. Good day."

Much as I enjoyed Holmes' withering assessment, I was also mindful of the state of our bank account, and so endeavoured to smooth things over.

"Holmes, I think what His Grace means is—"

"I know very well what he means," Holmes interrupted. "But why should I indulge the whims of every idle member of the nobility who shows up at our doorstep? I am a busy man."

Holmes moved to his desk and began rearranging some papers, not so much because they needed rearranging, but because he wanted to convey to our visitor his complete and utter disinterest in his case. Alarmed by Holmes' dismissive attitude, our distinguished guest deigned to turn and actually look at Holmes.

"I assure you, Mr. Holmes, this is a very serious matter. A matter of life and death."

"Oh dear," Holmes replied carelessly. "Well, in that case, the details of your life are quite easily read. Our housekeeper could do it."

"Your housekeeper? Surely you jest."

"Mrs. Hudson, would you be so kind as to offer up a few deductions regarding our guest?"

Miss Adler smiled, always up for a deductive duel with Holmes.

"I would be delighted."

For this, I got my notebook out, fairly certain that some kind of fireworks would be forthcoming. Miss Adler approached our guest and began circling him, looking him up and down in a manner that he clearly found unnerving as he fumbled to take off his gloves. Miss Adler took them from him, examined them, then examined his hands and his cane. The whole process couldn't have taken more than thirty seconds before she turned to Holmes.

"Married. English. But based upon his accent, one German parent, probably an emotionally distant father. Fluctuating facial asymmetry indicates the presence of inbreeding, most likely representing a union between two first cousins. Heavy smoker, right-handed, no evidence whatsoever of manual labour, but a slight callosity on the right forefinger indicates repeated use, probably from shooting a variety of guns. His ready access to an anonymous hansom cab suggests he has used it previously, most likely for visits to brothels or to facilitate adulterous affairs, but the absence of any obvious scars or contusions indicates he is of sufficient status that everyone ignores or accepts his compulsive philandering. Is there anything you would add, Mr. Holmes?"

Holmes left his desk and gave our guest a perfunctory glance.

"Only one trifle. Judging from his age, build, and the fact that the short trip up our stairs has produced a light sheen of sweat on his brow, I would deduce that his hobby of adulterous liaisons has come to an end recently, as he is now, in all likelihood, completely impotent."

It was all I could do to suppress a laugh, but our guest was far from amused.

"This is monstrous! How dare you?"

Keenly aware that a potentially large fee was about to walk out of our door in a state of high dudgeon, I rose to our guest's defence.

"Holmes, for God's sake! He's the Duke of Lancaster."

And at that, it was my turn to be surprised as Holmes burst into laughter and was immediately joined by Miss Adler.

"Yes, of course he is! And I am Long John Silver!" And for the first and last time in my life, I heard Holmes approximate a pirate accent. "Arr, matey! Shiver me timbers!"

"And I am Alice in Wonderland!" enthused Miss Adler. "This case is most definitely becoming curiouser and curiouser!"

"Who would you like to be, Watson?" asked Holmes. "Count Dracula? Dr. Frankenstein, perhaps? We may as well all assume fictional identities so we're on equal footing."

"This is outrageous! What is the meaning of this?" As Holmes had clearly intended, a nerve had been struck in our guest.

"You are certainly free to call yourself whatever you wish, Your Royal Highness, but why you should feel compelled to do so is utterly beyond me."

In an instant, our guest's outrage had left him and he appeared to be genuinely taken aback.

"You know who I am?"

"Of course!" replied Holmes. "You sir, are Albert Edward, The Prince of Wales. Son of Victoria and Albert, and first in line for the British Crown. Informally known as Bertie, and thanks to your prodigious appetite, even more informally known as Tum Tum."

Chapter Four

A Royal Pummelling

So there it was. The Prince of Wales himself. Given Miss Chartier's suggestive remarks regarding His Royal Highness during her visit, I shouldn't have been surprised to find him standing before me, but here he was in the quite considerable flesh. Clearly, Miss Chartier was responsible for this, manipulating events and people behind the scenes, but precisely how she had moved this particularly important piece into position was beyond me. The fact that she had been born the daughter of a master criminal and he had been born as heir to the British Crown was immaterial.

She wanted the Prince of Wales to arrive at our rooms at this particular point in time, and so here he was, in all of his faux military glory. While not of a particularly deterministic or fatalistic disposition, I couldn't help but feel that if Miss Chartier required Bertie's presence at Coney Island in New York on Christmas Day, he would somehow find himself there, even if he had no idea why. For his part, now that his true identity had been revealed, Bertie slowly removed his mask, genuinely crestfallen that his rather pedestrian disguise had failed to fool Sherlock Holmes.

"Yes, Mr. Holmes," he admitted. "You are quite correct. I am the Prince of Wales. Your reputation, and that of your extraordinary housekeeper are well deserved. But please don't call me Tum Tum."

I made a mental note not to call him Tum Tum to his face, but at the same time made another mental note to be sure to include that delicious detail in any recounting of the case. As for myself, I wouldn't say that I am of an unduly mercenary disposition, but my immediate thought was that the presence of royalty in our rooms upped the financial stakes considerably. If the heir to the British Crown needed Sherlock Holmes' help, I wanted to make sure that he received it, and I also wanted to make certain he recompensed us handsomely for our efforts.

Beyond that, it occurred to me that I wouldn't be averse to being called Sir John Watson at some future date, for services rendered to the Crown. What might those services be? I had no idea. But in that vein, I felt that a little buttering up wouldn't hurt, and so I bowed deeply in Bertie's direction.

"Your Majesty."

"No, Watson," Holmes corrected me, "not quite yet. But with Queen Victoria nearly eighty years old and about to celebrate her Diamond Jubilee, yes, it's fair to say that you are gazing upon the man who shall very soon be known as Edward the VII, King of England and Emperor of India."

"True," Bertie nodded his agreement, "but only if I can make it through today without being assassinated!"

"Well, I wish you the best of luck," replied Holmes dismissively. "As it happens, I have just been commissioned by Auguste Escoffier to clear up some difficulties at The Savoy Hotel, so I'm afraid I can't take your case at the moment."

"Holmes, he's the Prince of Wales!" I cried out, with visions of my knighthood rapidly disappearing. "If he's being threatened with assassination, you must help him!"

"Why?"

"Do you doubt my word?" asked Bertie. "Is that it? I assure you the threat is very real! My own mother, who is practically a recluse, has been the subject of no fewer than seven assassination plots, one by a hunchbacked dwarf!"

"You're making that up," said Miss Adler.

"Not at all. John William Bean, 1842," declared Holmes, who was then unable to resist showing off his prodigious knowledge regarding all things criminal. "However, his pistol was only loaded with paper and tobacco, so his death sentence was commuted to eighteen months in prison."

"Well then, if you'll pardon my saying so, Mr. Holmes, I have to agree with Dr. Watson. Surely the life of a future monarch is more important than Monsieur Escoffier's case."

"I beg to differ," replied Holmes. "Some lives are worth saving and some are not. I regret to say that the life of His Royal Highness falls into the latter category."

I had breathed a sigh of relief when Miss Adler offered her opinion, for if Holmes was occasionally inclined to disagree with me, he almost never contradicted Miss Adler. This had nothing to do whatever with his romantic feelings for her; rather, Miss Adler was a woman of considerable experience and nice judgement, which both Holmes and I had come to appreciate. Why he was being so obstinate in this case was a mystery, although I was quite sure he had his reasons.

I knew there was nothing that I could say to change his mind, so the only thing left to do was allow events to play out and hope for the best. Bertie, as might be expected, was considerably out of sorts at Holmes' remarks. For his entire life people had been falling all over themselves to cater to his every whim, and now, with his life threatened, the one man he had turned to for help had callously dismissed his pleas due to a previous engagement. Mustering up his dignity as best he could, Bertie attempted to remain calm and in control.

"I would like to know upon what basis you make such an extraordinary and insulting judgement upon my character."

"Be careful what you wish for," answered Holmes. "As an American, Mrs. Hudson has only a passing acquaintance with the fashions and foibles of England's ruling class. Watson, of course, is too decent a man to interest himself in those scurrilous affairs. Sadly, my profession necessitates an intimate knowledge of England's best and brightest, the so-called Upper Ten Thousand who contribute absolutely nothing to society, yet live lives of pampered comfort while surrounded by the slums of London. You sir, vain, shallow, vicious, self-absorbed, and childish, the so-called Playboy Prince, otherwise known as Edward the Caresser, are the leader of this debauched and depraved pack, and I daresay the world would be a better place without you in it."

To say I was shocked to hear Holmes speak in such a fashion was putting it mildly. Over the years we had dealt with any number of conniving, reprehensible criminals, and not once had I heard Holmes verbally eviscerate any of them in the way he had just described the Prince of Wales. I could see a vein beginning to throb in Bertie's temple, and given his bulk and lack of fitness, began to fear that a coronary event might spare his putative assassins the job of killing him. He was clearly pouring every ounce of his energy into controlling what he really wanted to say and do.

"I will not deny that I have strong animal passions and that I am fond of good living, but your ridiculous and offensive opinion of me is entirely unwarranted!"

Holmes was having none of it. It was a curious feature of Holmes' personality, that the more incensed and outraged a villain or client became, the more cool and measured were his responses. This was perhaps best exemplified by his treatment of the violent and murderous Dr. Grimesby Roylott in "The

Adventure of the Speckled Band." Roylott had attempted to intimidate Holmes by taking our fireplace poker and bending it with his bare hands, but then moments after he had stormed out, Holmes took the poker and proceeded to calmly straighten it out as if he were unfolding a newspaper. Therefore, when Holmes turned to me with a bland smile, I was prepared for this particular situation to escalate into realms for which I imagined Bertie was entirely unprepared.

"Watson, please be so kind as to fetch the letter 'A' from my Index. No need to read the full entry on His Royal Highness, just scan through it for any items that happen to catch your eye."

Pulling the volume from the shelves, I could feel my pulse quickening as I leafed through it rapidly. I felt every eye in the room upon me, even as I wondered what Holmes' biographical entry on Bertie would reveal that I didn't already know.

"Here we are," I began. "'Albert Edward, born 1841, spouse Alexandra of Denmark, six children, but only four still living—'"

"Skip down a bit," instructed Holmes.

"'Affair with Lady Harriet Mordaunt, who had a baby of dubious parentage, with Lady Harriet subsequently being declared insane and committed to an asylum. Affair with Lady Susan Vane-Tempest. When she became pregnant Edward ordered her to terminate the pregnancy and refused to see her. There is no record of any child and she died soon afterward.'"

"The handiwork, no doubt, of Bertie's personal physician, Dr. Oscar Clayton," added Holmes. "A doctor, yes, but more accurately a pimp and abortionist for Bertie. Knighted in 1882 for services to the Crown, I believe."

Miss Adler was staring at Bertie and shaking her head.

"What is wrong with you?"

Holmes turned to Miss Adler. "I'm afraid I can't speak with any authority on the behaviour of the upper class in America, but here in England debauchery is considered a healthy amusement for the gentlemen of Bertie's crowd. There are very specific rules, mind you, the first being to never divorce, because that would bring exposure and public disgrace. Beyond that, it's considered indecorous for ladies to have affairs before the birth of their first child, and Bertie does prefer married women because any pregnancies can then be attributed to their husbands. He is also unaccountably fond of pouring brandy over people's heads as a practical joke, which his victims pretend to enjoy because he is the Prince of Wales, and for some reason I'm not going to pretend that I understand, he takes an adolescent joy in risqué jokes involving umbrellas."

"It's all lies!" cried Bertie. "All of it! Complete fabrications concocted by my enemies and the press!"

"Ah, do you hear that?" Holmes cupped his hand to his ear for dramatic effect. "'It's all lies! The press are a pack of scoundrels! You can trust only me!' The cry of every loathsome despot down through the ages, and usually believed by his fearful and ignorant followers. Sadly, the facts tell a different tale, and as it happens I have a keen respect for accurate data and factual information."

With my nose still buried in Holmes' Index, I was aghast at just how much damning and appalling material there was regarding Bertie. It seemed to go on endlessly.

"'The Aylesford Scandal of 1876, the Tranby Croft Scandal of 1890'...good God..."

"You can stop, Watson," said Holmes. "I shall summarise. What you are gazing upon is a man born into money and privilege who has spent his entire life waiting for his mother to die. He has no sense of purpose, no vocation, and so he fills his days with smoking, gluttony, and liaisons with women from all classes of society. He races horses and yachts, and has private rooms at half the brothels in Europe, all of which is financed by the taxpayers of England to the tune of over one hundred thousand pounds per year, a sum which he feels he richly deserves."

"I do deserve it!" Bertie was floundering like a freshly speared sturgeon. "Do you have any idea of the number of luncheons I need to attend? The number of ribbons I cut on a weekly basis?"

With his eyes boring unwaveringly into Bertie, Holmes moved in for the kill. "And as you can see, he adores dressing up in uniform although he has never spent a day of military service in his life. Of course, the various courtiers and sycophants who surround him will never tell him what a miserable piece of human debris he is because they are all congenital cowards seeking to benefit from their association with him. In short, while he and his kind are a plague in almost every society, I present to you the sorriest example of upper-class vermin you are ever likely to meet."

"Seriously. What in God's name is wrong with you?" asked Miss Adler, disbelief and horror etched on her face.

Given world enough and time, I imagine that Holmes would have filled Miss Adler in on the various crimes and depravities routinely engaged in by Europe's ruling class, but it was at that moment that Bertie got to his feet, goaded beyond all endurance.

"Enough! You have insulted my honour, sir."

With one final twist of the knife, Holmes could barely keep the contemptuous sneer off his face. "If your honour is insulted by a simple recitation of facts then you never had any honour to begin with."

With his left eye beginning to twitch uncontrollably, Bertie proceeded to pick up one of his gloves, strode forward, then slapped Holmes across the face with it. "There! I challenge you to a duel, sir."

"Excellent," replied Holmes, as if he had just been invited to play a game of whist. "Then as the challenged party, I shall select our weapons. Watson, please be so kind as to fetch the box that you will find beneath my dresser."

As I was halfway there, I heard Holmes calling out further instructions. "And you may as well get your medical bag while you're at it."

Swiftly retrieving both, when I reentered the room I observed a cocky smile spreading across Bertie's face as he spotted the rattan case in my hands. "Duelling pistols, Mr. Holmes? You are making a serious mistake. As your housekeeper correctly deduced, I am quite experienced with guns. On my last trip to India I shot no fewer than twenty-nine tigers."

"How incredibly brave of you," returned Holmes. "I take it the tigers did not shoot back?"

Holmes nodded towards me. "Offer our guest first choice of weapon."

Putting my medical bag down, I opened the rattan box and showed it to Bertie, who looked inside with a smile at two pairs of boxing gloves.

"Boxing, eh? That suits me as well."

I directed what I hoped was an encouraging smile in Bertie's direction, but I knew beyond a certainty that the next few minutes would end any and all ambitions I had of receiving a knighthood or our bank account being improved by a generous royal dispensation. This was going to be a distinctly unpleasant experience for Bertie, and as I helped him off with his jacket, I mentally summoned up the image of where our cleaning supplies might be. It was true that there were some areas of personal combat where I might have embellished Holmes' abilities; for example, Holmes was not particularly adept with a sword, even if I had declared otherwise in "A Study in Scarlet." This, in fact, had contributed to him being humiliatingly chased about our rooms in "The Adventure of the Elusive Ear" by Marie Chartier, who had proved herself to be an expert fencer.

Boxing was another matter. Over the years, various cases had led us to a number of disreputable establishments near the wharves on the Thames or in the slums of London. Invariably, once our presence became known, some ruffian or other under the influence of a pint too many would challenge Holmes to a fight. I had yet to see Holmes turn down any such offer, with the result that I can relate with some accuracy the sound that dislodged teeth make as they skitter across a polished bar or the floor.

At first glance, Holmes did not appear to be an unduly exceptional athlete, but he was extraordinarily light on his feet, almost seeming to float across the ground, and he delivered his punches with stunning quickness and clinical accuracy, using his anatomical knowledge to paralyze his opponents with a blow to the liver, invariably followed up by a cross-hit under the jaw. In most cases, I felt as if I weren't so much watching a fight as witnessing a mathematical equation being solved. As I assisted Bertie in getting his gloves on, I looked across the room to see Miss Adler helping Holmes ready himself for combat.

"I'm going to enjoy putting you in your place, Mr. Holmes," taunted Bertie, looking at Holmes over my shoulder. "I've fought a few rounds in my time."

"No doubt against opponents specifically instructed not to fight back," returned Holmes. "But you are no longer in your pampered cocoon at Buckingham Palace or Marlborough House. You are now in the real world, where actions have consequences."

With both Bertie and Holmes prepared for battle, Miss Adler and I stepped out of the way, leaving the centre of the room clear for the carnage that was about to begin. Rapidly checking the contents of my medical bag, I was relieved to see a good assortment of bandages and ointments, along with smelling salts that would almost certainly be necessary in a minute or two. Bertie, with overweening confidence, proceeded to lumber straight towards Holmes like the overfed oaf that he was.

Holmes, up on the balls of his feet, feinted lightly left and right, and it was blazingly apparent that Bertie would never be able to lay a glove on him. Still, he tried gamely, taking one wild swing at Holmes and then following it up with another. Immediately recognising the lack of quality in his opponent, Holmes amused himself by hovering only an inch or two away from Bertie's most vicious punches. This went on for nearly a full minute, with Bertie beginning to gasp at his exertions, even as he kept flailing wildly away. Clearly growing bored with this ridiculous spectacle, Holmes turned his eye to Miss Adler.

"Behold the boxing style of the schoolyard bully, my dear. Wild, uncontrolled, and undisciplined. For myself, I prefer a more scientific approach. For example, I am aware that a bout with typhoid fever some years ago has given His Royal

Highness a bad left leg, and so I adopt a southpaw style to jab over his slow left hand..."

Changing his stance to put his right foot forward, Holmes proceeded to deliver a series of stinging jabs, dancing around Bertie the way a hound might torment a wounded bear. None of these punches were intended to incapacitate Bertie, they were merely to get his attention, and at this they succeeded splendidly. There was not only the shock of physical pain on Bertie's face, there was a growing terror behind his eyes. What was happening was not merely beyond his experience, it was beyond his imagination.

Bertie's occasional excursions into the world of boxing had given him the impression that he understood the sport and was capable of handling himself adequately well. With each of Holmes' punches, delivered at almost the speed of thought, the reality that Bertie thought he knew was crumbling to pieces. What was happening couldn't be happening, and yet as the blood began to trickle from his nose, there was the incontestable proof that it was, in fact, happening.

With Bertie now weaving in a daze in front of him, Holmes took a step back to survey his opponent, then turned to explain to Miss Adler what he was about to do next.

"...and now, disoriented, weary, with his vision blurred, it's a simple enough matter to despatch my opponent with what is perhaps my favourite punch, the cross-hit under the jaw."

I inwardly flinched. Surely he wouldn't. Bertie was practically out on his feet, and this was, after all, the Prince of Wales. However, Holmes was nothing if not consistent in his treatment of his fellow humans, from the highest of the high, to the lowest of the low. If he felt that a lesson needed to be imparted, he did not discriminate on the basis of class, and so I positioned myself two feet behind Bertie and waited for the inevitable, which wasn't long in coming. Holmes took one step forward and with a swift, compact motion, landed a powerful punch beneath Bertie's jaw, the force of it practically lifting Bertie into the air. As Bertie staggered back, out on his feet, I was able to catch him, and in one motion guided him into the armchair.

"Thus ever to tyrants," remarked Holmes as he eyed Bertie, apparently satisfied with his handiwork, before turning to me. "Your medical bag, I believe, Doctor."

As I cleaned His Royal Highness up, retrieved the smelling salts, and pulled the boxing gloves off Bertie's hands, I could see that Miss Adler was helping Holmes remove his gloves as well. I was immediately struck by the glowing expression on her face and the sparkle in her eyes. It was an odd thing, and one that I had witnessed several times in my lifetime, that while some women are instinctively repulsed by fighting and bloodshed, there are others who have a quite different, and I might add, more enthusiastic reaction to a violent scene of this sort.

At the bare-knuckle bouts that I sometimes attend, it is always easy to observe a handful of young men who have brought a sweetheart along with them, mindful of the stirring effects that a hard-fought match can have on even the most prim and proper young lady. Indeed, once she had Holmes' gloves off, Miss Adler grasped him firmly by the lapels and pulled him close.

"I know that I shouldn't enjoy witnessing a man being pummelled senseless, but my God that was wonderful!"

The ensuing kiss between them was, I daresay, of a rather passionate nature, and things would likely have continued in that vein had I not glanced at Bertie and observed that he was coming around. I forcibly cleared my throat and Holmes and Miss Adler both turned to see Bertie struggling to get back to his feet, still reeling from the effects of Holmes' thorough drubbing. With the primal instinct of the nobility, he made his way to our sideboard to pour himself a large glass of brandy.

"Mr. Holmes," he began, "I will not deny that I am possessed of certain failings. Certainly my youthful indiscretions are nothing to be proud of, but please be so kind to acknowledge that despite my status, I am quite ready to forget my rank—"

"—as long as everyone else remembers it," added Holmes.

"—that with my mother practically in seclusion, I have been the public face of the monarchy for the past thirty years—"

"—more's the pity."

"—and I am, when all is said and done, extremely punctual!"

Bertie raised his snifter to the ceiling, toasting himself and his punctuality, then proceeded to drain the glass.

"Well, that's something," I offered.

"True," Miss Adler agreed.

"So please help me!" Bertie pleaded, reaching for his jacket and pulling from one of the pockets an envelope identical to the one that Escoffier had left for Holmes. "I received this letter this morning…"

Holmes snatched the envelope away from Bertie, and as he and Miss Adler examined its contents, I assisted Bertie in getting his jacket back on.

"Aha!" began Holmes. "Once again we have the industrial paper…"

"…a broad-nibbed pen…" added Miss Adler.

"…and coarse, simple strokes."

"Monsieur Escoffier and His Royal Highness would appear to have the same correspondent."

"What does it say, Holmes?" I asked.

"It's quite short and to the point. 'You will not be in the parade for your mother's Diamond Jubilee tomorrow, for today you die. The Anarchists.'"

"Wonderful, Holmes! How do you know it's the Anarchists?"

Holmes tossed the note towards me. "That's how the letter is signed."

"But why would they want to kill the Prince of Wales?"

As Holmes struck a match to light his cherry-wood pipe, I could feel a lecture coming on, and was not disappointed.

"To bring an end to the British monarchy; indeed, to bring an end to all forms of government, which they see as hopelessly corrupt in an age where workers are paid poverty wages and one percent of the population owns over fifty percent of the wealth. And even with that wealth, when Bertie gambles away money at the Casino de Monte-Carlo or samples the pleasures to be had in the fleshpots of Baden, all of that is financed by the taxpayers of England.

"The Anarchists view the royal family as nothing more than a motley crew of gaudily attired parasites and leeches, and they are merely at the head of the long line of state beggars with noble titles. However, the scope of Anarchist activities is international. That's why they instigated the Haymarket Riot in Chicago, bombed the Liceu Opera House in Barcelona, and assassinated the French President only three years ago. Their motto is quite telling, 'A pound of dynamite is better than a bushel of bullets.'"

With a meditative puff, Holmes turned to Bertie. "But as you say, both your mother and you have received such threats in the past. You can surround yourself with the finest guards in Europe, so why come to me?"

"I don't trust them! I don't trust any of them," replied Bertie. "It only takes one traitor, and Anarchists fill the streets and sewers of London like rats. King Umberto of Italy was almost assassinated two months ago, and I fear that I am next. Beyond that, I was advised to seek your help."

For the first time since Bertie's entrance, I could see genuine interest in Holmes' face. "Really? By whom? Surely not Scotland Yard."

"No. It was a quite beautiful and brilliant woman I met at The Savoy Hotel."

"Do you have a name?"

And here, I am afraid that I simply couldn't resist the temptation now dangling before me. On countless occasions I have found myself gaping in wonder at some offhand comment or deduction by Holmes, and at long last here was an opportunity to return the favour. And so, in the most offhand and disinterested voice that I could manage, I casually drawled, "Unless I am greatly mistaken, I believe His Royal Highness must be referring to the Duchess of Killarney."

"Yes! Precisely!" Bertie was delighted to have me on his side. "She said she knew you, Dr. Watson, but my advisors have warned me against her."

"And now you fear that your very own advisors are part of a plot to betray you," I continued.

"Exactly! I have enemies everywhere! Thank you, Dr. Watson!"

Was that the renewed possibility of a knighthood I saw glimmering on the horizon? Perhaps. But even more delicious than the prospect of becoming Sir John Watson was the utter confusion and consternation on Holmes' face.

"What? Who is this woman? I've never heard of her."

This was too perfect, and a situation I felt sure would never arise again, so there was only one thing for it, to play it to the hilt.

"The Duchess of Killarney, of course. Do try to keep up, Holmes. It's all quite...what's the word? Elementary."

Out of the corner of my eye I saw Miss Adler stifle a laugh as Holmes looked genuinely taken aback. He clearly knew that something was amiss, but in the heat of the moment he didn't have time to orient himself and put me firmly in my place, as Bertie was warming to the subject of the very fictional Duchess of Killarney.

"I assure you, Mr. Holmes, the Duchess is quite unlike any woman I have ever met. Beautiful, brilliant, and beyond charming. She has this dark fire in her eyes and do you know, when we first encountered one another last week, she was so delighted that she asked me for both an autograph and a photograph. She seemed instinctively drawn to me, much in the manner that—"

"—flies are drawn to excrement, yes, I understand perfectly," added Holmes acerbically. "However, it's the one thing I don't understand that intrigues me most..."

Holmes turned and fixed me with his most penetrating gaze as I feigned obliviousness. "...and so I will take your case, Your Royal Highness."

"Thank you, Mr. Holmes! And please, do call me Bertie. Is there anything else I can tell you?"

"No, I appear to be quite out of my depth at the moment. On the other hand...Watson? You seem to be well up on things. Perhaps you have a question or two for Bertie."

This now called for the most delicate judgement on my part. Having roused the hound in Holmes from hibernation, it wouldn't do to poke him again. Rather, a fresh scent would be just the thing, and I was well aware that Miss Chartier had quite intentionally provided a trail for us to pick up and follow. Whether or not it had anything to do with her real object had yet to be determined, but it was all that we had at the moment. Summoning up my most casual tone, I addressed Bertie.

"Well, actually, I did have one thought. This being your mother's Diamond Jubilee and all, it got me to wondering, just out of idle curiosity, does Queen Victoria happen to own any significant diamonds herself?"

"Why yes," returned Bertie. "She owns the Koh-i-Noor."

"The what?"

"The famed Koh-i-Noor Diamond," explained Miss Adler. "Koh-i-Noor is a Persian phrase, it means Mountain of Light, and at over one hundred carats, it's one of the largest and most valuable diamonds in the world." She paused, a distinct twinkle in her eye. "Are you certain that your question was prompted entirely by idle curiosity, Dr. Watson?"

"What can I say? I'm a curious fellow."

"To put it mildly," observed Holmes drily. He then turned to Bertie. "Well, given the nature of the threats that may be lurking outside these rooms, I suggest that you not leave our company for the remainder of the day."

"Gladly!" agreed Bertie. "I feel safer here than I would under armed guard at Buckingham Palace. But please, for the love of God, tell me you have something to eat. I'm absolutely famished. What does your housekeeper specialise in?"

I must admit I perked up at this. Various visitors had met our "housekeeper" Mrs. Hudson, but this was the first time any of them had requested food. Holmes, too, seemed nonplussed by Bertie's question.

"Ah...I'm afraid that Mrs. Hudson doesn't actually prepare meals, as it were."

"What the devil do you mean? That's absurd!" In his hunger and outrage, Bertie turned his full attention to Miss Adler. "Do you seriously mean to tell me that—hold on now...I recognise your face! Surely, you're...why yes, it's Irene Adler, the American contralto! I saw the premiere of your performance in 'Esmeralda' at the Theatre Royal. But aren't you supposed to be—"

"No, I'm not dead, it's a long story, I will thank you for your discretion, and no, I don't cook."

It took Bertie a few moments to process this information, and I was curious as to what his reaction would be. Surprise at the resurrection of a dead American opera singer? Disbelief that the ostensibly celibate and monastic Sherlock Holmes had taken up residence with his lover? In the end, predictably enough, Bertie returned to the only thing that really mattered to him; that is, the empty condition of his stomach.

"But you're a woman! You must cook something...veal, perhaps? A nice loin of pork or lamb? With a demi-glace sauce and roasted potatoes?"

"I don't cook. Anything. Ever," returned Miss Adler with a patient smile.

"Unbelievable…" Bertie stared at her, aghast. Miss Adler could have revealed herself to be one of the Gorgons, with snakes writhing atop her head, and Bertie would not have been more flummoxed and appalled. "Completely and totally...this is why England is going to the dogs! Women want to smoke, women want to ride bicycles, women want to vote for God's sake, and now they can't even cook!"

"You don't think women should vote?" asked Miss Adler, with a dangerous look in her eye.

"Don't be ridiculous! Women voting? That's madness! They're too ignorant! Too emotional! For God's sake, at some point every month women go completely insane!"

As terrified as Bertie was about assassination-minded Russian Anarchists in the streets, if he'd any sense at all he would have been much more worried about Miss Adler, who I was alarmed to see had just wrapped her hand around the hilt of the sword located amongst our fireplace tools.

"Holmes..." she began.

"Steady..."

"It is my birthday..."

"I shall make it up to you. I promise."

Their eyes met, and to my considerable relief, Miss Adler released her grip on the sword. Bertie was oblivious to all this, because the condition of being hungry was such a rare occurrence for him that he was starting to panic.

"This is not going to work! I can't possibly be expected to live like this. Perhaps a quick run out to The Savoy...I'll just have three or four courses...and one of Escoffier's most excellent soufflés for dessert."

"If you value your life," counselled Holmes, "I don't recommend leaving these rooms."

Bertie was already putting on his gloves. "I'm sorry, Mr. Holmes, but I simply must have some decent food!"

"Watson, since you still have the 'A' Index close at hand, kindly read Bertie the entry on Czar Alexander II of Russia. I think he might find it most instructive."

Picking up the Index, I rapidly located the section on Alexander II, and looked to Holmes for further instruction.

"You can skip right to the end."

Locating the final paragraph, I began reading. "'Czar Alexander II was assassinated by Russian Anarchists on March 13, 1881. When the bomb exploded over twenty people were injured, and...'" I paused, my stomach turning at the words in front of me.

"Go on," urged Holmes.

"'...Alexander's legs were torn off, his stomach ripped open, his face a mask of agony as he bled to death.'"

I looked at Bertie, who had gone completely still and was a shade whiter. Somewhere deep inside he was calculating the pleasure to be had ingesting one of Escoffier's soufflés as opposed to the very real possibility of being blown to pieces by an Anarchist's bomb. At the very least, it spoke volumes for the quality of a soufflé prepared by Escoffier himself, and I made a mental note to try one at the earliest opportunity.

It was at this critical juncture, just as I was wondering if Bertie would make a dash for the stairs and whether or not Holmes would forcibly restrain him that our door opened and Marie Chartier entered, bearing a covered dish. Beautifully coiffed and attired in a vibrant green dress, with a plunging neckline guaranteed to draw the full attention of Bertie, she looked around the room with the easy smile of a simple Irish lass, and I recognised immediately that I was gazing upon Miss Chartier's alter-ego, the Duchess of Killarney herself.

Chapter Five

The Duchess of Killarney Weaves Her Web

The sudden appearance of Marie Chartier had an electric effect on everyone in the room, although for much different reasons. Holmes and Miss Adler quickly stood up, ready for anything from the brilliant and wicked daughter of Professor Moriarty. On the other hand, Bertie's face was a picture of giddy delight, as he found himself not only in the presence of the beautiful Duchess of Killarney, but she also appeared to be bearing a plate of food.

For myself, knowing both her true identity and her assumed one, I could only wait to see how she would present herself to us and how her scheme would unfold. I didn't have long to wait, as she addressed us with a rich Irish brogue.

"I'm terribly sorry to interrupt. I knocked but there was no answer—oh, Your Royal Highness! I was hoping to find you here! And Dr. Watson! Aren't you a sight for sore eyes! It's been too long!"

"Indeed it has," I agreed, feeling a bit guilty at playing along, but enjoying myself nevertheless.

Bertie could barely contain himself. "Duchess! Yes, I took your advice! Mr. Holmes, this is the woman I spoke to you about—the Duchess of Killarney!" He then turned his attention back to Miss Chartier. "Mr. Holmes has agreed to help me!"

As she swept further into the room, every eye was on her. "How wonderful! I was hoping he would, but then a terrible thought occurred to me. In reading Dr. Watson's marvellous stories, I know that Sherlock Holmes doesn't eat when he's on a case. Well, I knew that would never do for my Bertie, so I stopped by The Savoy Hotel and had Chef Escoffier prepare you some food."

"Escoffier himself?" Bertie clapped his hands together in delight, like a small child who has been told that Christmas will come one day early. "But how is that possible? He has an entire kitchen to run!"

"I can be very persuasive..." Miss Chartier held the covered plate beneath Bertie's nose. "...and so I have your favourite dish."

"Impossible!" Bertie exclaimed. "Poularde Derby? Chicken stuffed with truffles and foie gras? And surrounded by more truffles cooked in champagne and slices of foie gras on a small crouton of bread fried in butter?"

In response, Miss Chartier offered her most seductive smile and slowly uncovered the dish. If any woman ever owned any man's mind, body, and soul, it was Miss Chartier in that moment as Bertie took in the intoxicating scents of the dish and swooned with delight. Never the brightest Prince in Europe, the combination of Miss Chartier and the Poularde Derby had the cumulative effect of addling Bertie's senses to the point that he could do little more than gape at her in awe.

"It's heaven! I'm in heaven, you beautiful, beautiful creature! Isn't she wonderful? But I really am feeling quite faint, I must lie down for a moment."

Remarkably, during all of this, neither Holmes nor Miss Adler had moved a muscle. Rather, they had focused their attention entirely on Miss Chartier, although in slightly different ways. For Holmes, he was fixated on her every movement, the way an audience watches a magician, determined to see what the trick is, even as the magician skillfully misdirects the eye to achieve an amazing result. Miss Adler was similarly enthralled, but in her eyes I read the wariness of a snake charmer confronted with a weaving cobra. I had already seen Miss Adler glance towards the sword amongst our fireplace tools, and I had no doubt she had calculated just how quickly she could get it in her hand.

As for Miss Chartier, fully immersed in her character of the Duchess of Killarney, she pretended not to notice the effect that her arrival had had on everyone else save Bertie. Even now, as Bertie declared his light-headedness, her countenance took on an expression of the most solicitous concern imaginable.

"Oh, my poor Bertie! What a day you have had, but you have been so, so brave to come and consult with Mr. Holmes! Let me just take you to one of the bedrooms for a few moments, with your chicken, of course! And don't you worry, Chef Escoffier himself will be bringing more food quite soon."

"There is a God above! Thank you, my angel..."

Still carrying the dish, and with a steadying hand on Bertie's elbow, Miss Chartier moved him towards Holmes' bedroom. In turn, both Miss Chartier and Bertie glanced back at us before they exited. In Miss Chartier's eyes I read nothing less than the look of a fox dragging a hapless rabbit down into its lair. As for Bertie, I could see the wild hope that once he had wolfed down his Poularde Derby, that he would have the opportunity to be alone with Miss Chartier and press his affections upon her.

In a moment, they were gone and the door was closed, leaving Bertie and Miss Chartier to their own devices. Meanwhile, now alone with Holmes and Miss Adler, I resigned myself to the fact that we were about to have our own little drama. Ignoring me completely, Holmes turned to Miss Adler.

"Is it just me, or does the Duchess of Killarney bear a striking similarity to Marie Chartier?"

"There is a marked resemblance," agreed Miss Adler.

"And here's a peculiar thing…" Holmes picked up one of the sherry glasses that I had put on the sideboard, looking at it closely from all angles. "I believe you had left the room, my dear, when Watson related how he and Escoffier had drunk a toast to the scrambled eggs. Now then, my memory's not quite what it used to be, but I don't recall Monsieur Escoffier wearing this particular shade of red lipstick..."

Eager to join in, Miss Adler picked up her black negligee from the divan and held it under Holmes' nose, "And here's another peculiar thing. This is my negligee, but I don't use this particular perfume..."

"Phul-Nana by Grossmith's of London," determined Holmes. "The notes of geranium, neroli, and sandalwood are quite distinctive."

"And coincidentally enough," added Miss Adler, "as the Duchess of Killarney just passed by me, I believe I detected the faint fragrance of Phul-Nana perfume..."

"...not to mention her striking red lips, bearing a hue remarkably similar to the one on this sherry glass," concluded Holmes.

Having duly delighted themselves with their own cleverness and established quite conclusively that Marie Chartier and I had enjoyed a private conference in their absence, they then turned to me, no doubt expecting some kind of humiliating confession on my part at being seduced and hoodwinked by Miss Chartier. However, I was ready for them, and I returned their accusing looks with a calm and steady gaze.

"Well, this is all part of my plan, obviously."

As this was the last thing they expected to hear, Holmes and Miss Adler exchanged a perplexed look.

"Do tell," said Holmes.

"Marie Chartier stopped by while you two were out and hinted at a most incredible scheme involving Chef Escoffier and the Prince of Wales. So, rather than chasing her all over London endeavouring to somehow uncover the crime she has in mind, I thought it was best that I pose as her confederate and bring her here, where we might expose her plan and put a stop to the whole business!" I paused for dramatic effect. "You're welcome."

Holmes and Miss Adler looked at one another again, and I would no doubt have been buffeted by questions from all sides, if not for the fact that at that very moment, there was the sound of a door closing, and we all turned to see Miss Chartier reentering the room. With Bertie safely ensconced in the bedroom and presumably elbows-deep in his chicken, Miss Chartier felt free to abandon her character of the Duchess of Killarney, and so she addressed us with her familiar French accent.

"Well, well, well. And so we meet again. You are looking well, Mr. Holmes. And you, Miss Adler. Always a pleasure. Bertie is resting comfortably with his chicken. Poor thing."

"Bertie is a pig," rejoined Miss Adler.

"Of course he is. You think I do not know that?"

"Then that's one thing we agree on, but I suspect the only thing. So let me say straight out, Miss Chartier, that while I know Mr. Holmes enjoys these intellectual duels, I'm afraid I don't have the patience for that." Miss Adler plucked the sword from the fireplace tools and pointed it directly at Miss Chartier's throat. "What are you up to? Out with it!"

Miss Chartier, with the sangfroid I had come to expect from her, didn't panic in the least at having a razor sharp blade inches from her jugular vein. Instead, she gazed calmly down the length of the sword and then looked straight into Miss Adler's eyes. "There is no need to threaten me. I am perfectly happy to tell you what I am up to. I am going to assassinate the Prince of Wales in the rooms of Sherlock Holmes."

Needless to say, this was the most memorable announcement ever made within my hearing. I was struggling for different ways to interpret it, searching for some kind of metaphor or hidden meaning, but I was failing miserably as Miss Adler sought to confirm the evidence of her own ears.

"What? I'm sorry, what did you just say?"

"I am going to kill Bertie."

If Miss Chartier's declaration had been nothing less than stunning, Miss Adler's response equalled it.

"Well, get a sword. Let's do this."

Now it was Miss Chartier's turn to be taken aback. "Excuse me?"

"I'll help you kill the bastard," clarified Miss Adler.

Feeling as if I had entered some form of alternate reality to hear the murder of the Prince of Wales spoken about in such a cavalier fashion, I turned to Holmes and was gratified to see that he appeared to be as aghast as I was.

"Irene, may I point out that assassinating the Prince of Wales in our rooms might not be in the best interests of our business?"

"You're right. So, we'll have to kill him somewhere else, then dump his body in the Thames." Seeing Holmes' shocked expression, Miss Adler pointed to his Index. "I could randomly put my finger anywhere on your entry on Bertie and find reason enough to put a bullet through him or push him off a bridge. He's a horrible human being who uses his position and privilege to ruin the lives of other people, especially women. You just said it yourself before you beat the living tar out of him—the world would be a better place without him in it."

While Holmes and I may have been unprepared for Miss Adler's homicidal inclinations towards His Royal Highness, Miss Chartier nodded approvingly. "I am liking you more and more, Miss Adler."

At this point, I felt obliged to intervene as my mind ran back to an earlier conversation. "I say, Miss Chartier, I asked you quite directly if anyone would be hurt by your scheme and you said no!"

"That is quite true," she replied matter-of-factly. "He won't be hurt. He will be blown to pieces."

"So you're an Anarchist?" asked Miss Adler.

"Don't be ridiculous! I am the most capitalistic person you will ever meet. I have been hired by the Anarchists to kill him."

While I was relieved to hear that Miss Chartier was not an Anarchist, and mindful of all the benefits that capitalism brings to any society by way of healthy competition and rugged individualism, to my way of thinking capitalism that extends to murdering other human beings for your own profit is taking things just a bit too far. I realise that some of the American robber barons, such as the late Jay Gould, might scoff at my sensitivity on that score, but there it is.

"Well, call me prudish if you like," I objected, "but I want to go on record as saying that I object to any plan that involves blowing up the Prince of Wales!"

"That's very patriotic of you, Watson," said Holmes, "but if I might put a slight damper on the level of bloodlust in the room, I would point out one curious fact regarding His Royal Highness."

"What's that?"

"He's not dead yet."

Of course, Holmes was absolutely right. Whether days earlier at The Savoy Hotel or here in our rooms, Miss Chartier had already had ample opportunity to bring the life of His Royal Highness to a premature end. In fact, it would have been ludicrously easy for her to lure Bertie to a private room at The Savoy under the pretence of an intimate assignation, at which point she could have despatched him in whatever fashion suited her fancy. It was then, for a mad moment or two, that it occurred to me that she had already killed Bertie.

Either by silently throttling him or feeding him chicken laced with potassium cyanide, the heir to the British Crown might already be a rapidly cooling corpse in Holmes' bedroom. However, before I had a chance to say a word or rush to check on His Royal Highness, the bedroom door opened and Bertie emerged looking quite hale and hearty as he licked chicken grease from his fingers.

"Delicious! Absolutely delicious! You know what someone should do? Invent a business where you deliver food to people's houses!"

And then, like a honeybee spying a beautiful orchid, Bertie headed directly for Miss Chartier before Holmes stepped in his path and took him by the shoulders.

"Bertie, there's something I think you should know about your new friend, the Duchess of Killarney."

Even with Holmes standing right in front of him, Bertie didn't hear a word that Holmes said, as he only had eyes for Miss Chartier. "In fact, my dear Duchess, was I hearing things, or did you say that Chef Escoffier would be arriving with more food?"

Keeping true to her character as the Duchess, Miss Chartier once again assumed an Irish brogue. "Oh yes indeed! And I do believe he'll be bringing some of Your Royal Highness' favourite dishes."

"Wonderful! Well, this vigil won't be quite as excruciating as I imagined after all! Especially if the Duchess will consent to favour us with her quite exquisite presence for just a bit longer."

Bertie was now literally trying to force Holmes out of the way so that he could get to Miss Chartier, but Holmes is not a man easily moved if he chooses to stand his ground. Taking an even stronger grip on Bertie, Holmes made another attempt to penetrate the fog of lust that had descended upon His Royal Highness.

"Yes, but before the gorging begins I feel obliged to inform you that you are under a severe misapprehension regarding the Duchess here. In point of fact, she is actually—"

"No, no, no! I can't abide small talk before I have dined properly!" Abandoning his efforts to go through Holmes, Bertie spun away in the opposite direction, at which point he spotted our new Edison Home Phonograph in the corner of the room and his eyes went wide.

"I say, is that one of Thomas Edison's newfangled phonograph machines? Excellent! Let's have a little music, shall we? What do we have here?" Bertie removed the cylinder from the machine and peered at it closely. "Ah, 'The Blue Danube' waltz! Wonderful!"

Before anyone could interfere, Bertie had wound the machine up and the strains of Johann Strauss' "The Blue Danube" filled the room. Offering his hand to Miss Chartier, she took it with a graceful curtsy, and they began waltzing around the furniture. Grateful for a small reprieve from all of the tension in the room, I saw no reason why I shouldn't join in, and so I extended my hand to Miss Adler, and a moment later we were dancing as well.

This, of course, left Holmes on his own, and as I cast a glance in his direction, he was frowning, with his arms crossed, and making it quite clear that he was not at all pleased with how events were unfolding. On the one hand, I understood his frustration. Normally, he was the orchestrator of all events that took place in 221B, and here he had found himself supplanted by not only the Prince of Wales, but by Marie Chartier in the guise of the Duchess of Killarney and up to who knows what? On the other hand, as was often the case, I felt that a little perspective might do Holmes good, and I said as much to Miss Adler.

"Oh dear. Look at him. Holmes is miffed at me. You'd think he'd have the decency to be a little grateful."

"For...?"

"He's the one always moaning that he doesn't have any good cases! 'Where have all the master criminals gone?' he says. Right, here you are then!"

"Well, he doesn't like surprises," pointed out Miss Adler.

"What are the stories called? 'The *Adventures* of Sherlock Holmes,' yes? What do adventures tend to include? Surprises!"

And it was at that very moment that I received a considerable surprise of my own. Holmes came towards us, tapped Miss Adler on the shoulder to cut in, and a moment later I found myself waltzing away with the world's foremost consulting detective.

"Oh, hello, Holmes," I managed, wondering what on earth he could be thinking.

"Hello, Watson," he returned, as if he and I waltzing were a regular occurrence. "I say, old fellow, may I ask you a question?"

"Of course."

But before Holmes could say another word, we both became aware of Bertie quite intentionally waltzing Miss Chartier in the direction of Holmes' bedroom. Sure enough, a moment later he had ushered Miss Chartier through the door, and then had the unmitigated effrontery to beckon Miss Adler to join them. Happily, her outraged look gave Bertie all the answer he needed, and with a smile and shrug of good grace, he followed Miss Chartier and closed the bedroom door behind him. Holmes turned back to me, his demeanour a touch more direct now that Bertie was out of the room.

"What the hell are you up to?"

"I'm not entirely sure."

"Shall I tell you what it looks like to me? It would appear that you are collaborating with the most dangerous criminal in Europe to commit the crime of the century. You dance beautifully, by the way."

"Thank you," I replied, genuinely flattered that Holmes had complimented my waltzing. "And I tried to tell you that Miss Chartier had been here while you and Miss Adler were out!"

"You never did!"

"Of course I did, but you were too busy being clever to listen to me! It's always the same! 'Oh, do note the coarse writing paper!' 'Oh, do note the broad-nibbed pen!' Then you two were all over one another. I couldn't get a word in edgewise!"

Just as our conversation was on the verge of getting even more heated, our attention was drawn by the sound of a slap and a yelp of pain from the bedroom.

"Crivens!" we heard Bertie cry out.

Any concerns that I had about Bertie meeting his demise were quelled a moment later, as Miss Chartier emerged from the bedroom with a small smile, still swaying to the music, and all was made clear. Evidently, Bertie had made some sort of unwelcome advance towards her, and she had expressed her disinterest in the only way Bertie would understand. With that settled, I could see Holmes preparing to lecture me, but with impeccable timing Miss Adler swooped in and waltzed away with him. With a sympathetic audience now quite literally in his arms, Holmes couldn't restrain himself from having a bit of a moan.

"It's hopeless! I don't know what to do with Watson sometimes. People think I'm hard to live with? They should try living with a writer! No principles, no moral compass, it's all about the damned story!"

"Sweetheart, you're overreacting—"

"Overreacting? In a few minutes we're going to have the Prince of Wales' brains all over our walls!"

"Well, look at the bright side," soothed Miss Adler. "That won't be a very big mess."

Holmes smiled, then laughed, with Miss Adler joining him.

"That's a good one," said Holmes. "I like that."

"You're welcome," Miss Adler continued. "Now let me be the one to tell Bertie that the Duchess of Killarney doesn't really exist."

As Holmes was about to object, she placed a finger on his lips. "You can be a little abrupt sometimes. We don't want

93

Bertie to panic and do something stupid. I will let him down as gently as possible."

With the music winding down, Bertie emerged from the bedroom twirling his moustache and resumed his pursuit of Miss Chartier. I had imagined that he might be slightly chastened by his recent experience with her, but if anything, her combative and resistant nature had only served to sharpen his appetite, as it were.

Presumably, with practically every noblewoman in the country at his beck and call, the thrill of the hunt now compelled him to stalk Miss Chartier with a single-minded fervour that bordered on obsession. While I might have feared for the prospect of any other woman in these circumstances, that was most definitely not true of Miss Chartier, who was more than capable of deflecting His Royal Highness' advances.

As he reached for her, she spun away and launched into an Irish jig worthy of a native of Dublin. With her upper body perfectly still and her feet merely a blur as she kicked and whirled, she ended her impromptu performance with a low curtsy, causing Bertie to wildly applaud her efforts. Holmes, Miss Adler, and I immediately joined in as well, because it had been as impressive as it was unexpected, and I began to get an inkling of just how much thought and effort she had put into the creation of her Duchess of Killarney character.

"Marvellous, my dear!" Bertie gushed. "Absolutely marvellous! The finest Irish jig I have ever seen in my life! You are a superb dancer!"

Seeing her opening, Miss Adler approached Bertie and took him by the arm. "Indeed she is. And dancing is only one of the Duchess of Killarney's many, many talents. In fact, she is even more remarkable than you imagine."

"Do tell, Miss Adler! I want to know everything about her! I am absolutely smitten! Smitten, I say! Nothing you say will surprise me."

"No? Well, you might want to sit down for this because—"

But before Miss Adler could reveal Miss Chartier for who she really was, our door burst open and Chef Escoffier himself entered carrying a tray with several covered dishes on it. With the unbridled hubris I had come to expect of the man, he paused just inside the door, thrust his chin into the air, and announced, "Escoffier is here!!! And he comes bearing the fruits of his genius!"

Again, Bertie burst into applause. "Wonderful! I must say Duchess, you clearly have Chef Escoffier completely under your spell. What's your secret?"

"Oh, it's very simple, I assure you," she replied in her Irish brogue, directing a meaningful glance at Escoffier. "My secret is that I keep my secrets...don't I, Auguste?"

"Of course, of course!" Whatever designs Escoffier may have had on a more intimate relationship with Miss Chartier after making her acquaintance, it was clear that a recent conference between them had put matters in a different light, and he was now doing everything in his power to do her bidding and keep her happy.

"Now then, what have you brought us, my good man?" Bertie was rubbing his hands together in anticipation as he ran his eyes over the covered dishes on the tray.

"Allow me," began Escoffier. "Dr. Watson, if you would be so kind." Handing me the tray, Escoffier began to point to the dishes one by one.

"We have, of course, the Canapés au Caviar, the Stewed Turtle Fins finished with Madeira Port, and a special little dish of mine that I like to call *Cuisses de Nymphes à l'Aurore.*"

"Thighs of Nymphs at Dawn?" interjected Miss Adler.

"*Exactement!*"

"What on earth is that?" I asked.

"Frog legs!"

"Oh my God..."

"Poached in court bouillon in a sauce flavored with paprika and tarragon. Ah, but the *pièce de résistance*, of course, can only be one dish and one dish alone."

"It can't be..." Bertie was practically salivating by this point.

"Oh, but it is!" Escoffier assured him. "Prepare yourself, Your Royal Highness."

I can only describe what followed as falling somewhere between an elaborate dining ritual and a religious rite. Both Bertie and Escoffier knew their roles and followed them with an almost military precision. First, Bertie sat on the divan with his chin up and outthrust. Escoffier proceeded to hand him a large linen napkin, which Bertie then stuffed inside the front of his shirt collar.

From there, things got more and more strange. Escoffier produced a second large linen napkin, and my expectation was that he would drape it across Bertie's lap. Instead, however, he held the napkin by two corners, snapped it into the air, and as Bertie bowed his head, allowed the napkin to settle lightly over Bertie's head, obscuring His Royal Highness completely from our view. Feeling entirely out of my depth, I looked to Holmes and Miss Adler, only to see that they were as baffled by these proceedings as I was. Taking in our mystification, Escoffier allowed himself a small smile.

"Ah, I see your confusion, my friends. It is only natural..." Escoffier picked up the final covered dish on the tray and held it before us. "...for this is the rarest dish in the world. Delicate, sublime, illegal in many countries, yes, but a favourite of His Royal Highness when it can be procured on the black market."

With his vision completely obscured by the napkin over his head, Bertie had both hands out before him, clutching at the empty air in his frantic attempts to take the dish from Escoffier, who only smiled, apparently used to this humiliating spectacle.

"Patience, Your Royal Highness. Let the anticipation build..."

"Why does he have a napkin over his head?" I asked.

"To help retain the aromas of the dish once it is uncovered..." Escoffier explained as he slipped the dish beneath Bertie's napkin and onto his lap, "...and also, so they say, to hide one's shame from God."

"What the devil is it?"

"Ortolan. A tiny, delicate, beautiful little songbird...no larger than my thumb. Caught in nets, they are kept in total darkness so they overeat, and then they are drowned in a vat of Armagnac brandy, then roasted whole. You uncover the dish..." Escoffier reached beneath the napkin to remove the cloche, "...take in the intoxicating scent..." From beneath the napkin came a moan of pleasure from Bertie.

"...and then place the entire bird in your mouth. When you bite down you hear the crunch of the bones and feel the hot flesh and innards sliding down your throat. You chew slowly, grinding the skin, the bones pricking the inside of your cheeks so that your own warm blood mingles with the fat that tastes of hazelnuts. And now, Your Royal Highness, *bon appétit!*"

From beneath the napkin came an audible crunching sound, which instantly set my teeth on edge as I observed Holmes wincing in disgust. For her part, Miss Adler was unable to hide her horror at what was happening.

"Oh my God!!!"

Taking a swing at Bertie, she succeeded in knocking the napkin off his head, which he barely noticed. He was chewing slowly, eyes closed, a beatific smile on his face, as Miss Adler turned her attention to Escoffier.

"And you!"

Another wild swing from Miss Adler sent Escoffier's toque spinning across the room.

"*Mon Dieu!* She has gone mad!"

As Escoffier scrambled to recover his toque, Miss Adler looked at Miss Chartier and pointed to Bertie.

"Just do it! Kill him! Kill him now!"

This managed to get Bertie's attention and his eyes opened, although his chewing never slowed as Miss Adler advanced towards him.

"She's not an Irish Duchess, you damned fool! She's a professional assassin who has been hired to kill you because this is what you get after centuries of inbreeding between congenital idiots! A future king with the brains of a demented squirrel, whose sick, debauched, parasitic society needs a bullet through the head! It needs to burn to the ground, do you hear me? It needs to burn! Burn!! Burn!!!"

Coming up behind her, Holmes put his arms around Miss Adler, which was just as well, as she seemed to be on the verge of tearing the throat out of the confused Bertie.

"Well..." began Holmes, "...thank you for letting him down gently, dear."

Breathing heavily from her outburst, Miss Adler gently disengaged herself from Holmes' grasp, but just as I was mentally cataloguing which objects in the room she could use to kill Bertie, she held both hands up and took a step back from His Royal Highness.

"I'm going to need a minute."

As Miss Adler disappeared into her bedroom, Bertie dabbed at his lips with his napkin and looked around in genuine bewilderment.

"I've missed something, haven't I?" He turned to Miss Chartier. "You're not actually an assassin, are you? No, this is some kind of practical joke, it must be! Auguste, you know her. She's the Duchess of Killarney from The Savoy Hotel!"

"Well, I most certainly thought she was a Duchess, I did!" returned Escoffier. "Until she made matters very clear to me..."

"...and gave you a specific set of instructions which you are now carrying out in an effort to save your career and reputation," said Holmes.

"Speaking of which, Auguste..." Miss Chartier looked intently at Escoffier, who instantly understood her meaning.

"Yes, of course! Dessert! It is coming!"

Taking the tray of dishes with him, Escoffier made for the door at speed as Miss Chartier called out in her Irish brogue, "And some refreshments would be lovely!"

"Yes, yes! Anything you say!"

A moment later, Escoffier could be heard clattering down the stairs as Bertie endeavoured to process everything that had just transpired. Sadly for him, Miss Chartier had it exactly right when she said that he was one of those unfortunate people for whom the truth is much less important that what he wished the truth to be.

"There, you see! She has an Irish accent!" began Bertie. "She can dance an Irish jig, for God's sake! She's Irish!"

"I'm afraid not," countered Holmes. "Bertie, may I introduce you to Marie Chartier, daughter of the late Professor Moriarty, and the most dangerous woman in Europe."

"No," Bertie was adamant. "I'm sorry, I simply refuse to believe it."

"What?" I could scarcely believe that this was the future King of England sitting in front of me. "Good God, man! Whether or not you believe in something has nothing to do with whether it's true or not."

"Well, that's your opinion," returned Bertie.

"Yes, and my opinion is based on factual information, while yours is based on ineffable twaddle! They're hardly equal!"

"Well, I choose not to believe it and I am the Prince of Wales. So there."

And there the matter would have stayed, with the delusional Bertie believing whatever it pleased him to believe, save for the fact that having played her cards perfectly so far, Miss Chartier apparently was prepared to move on to the next stage of her plan, a stage that no longer required the existence of the fictional Duchess of Killarney.

Chapter Six

The Prince is Dead, Long Live the Prince!

As Bertie had been declaring his unwavering devotion to the demonstrably fictional Duchess of Killarney, the demonstrably nonfictional Marie Chartier was regarding Bertie the way I imagine a scientist scrutinises a newly discovered microorganism beneath his microscope. Despite her considerable experience manipulating men to her own advantage across Europe, it was evident she had never met anyone quite like the Prince of Wales, who clearly took a certain pride in being as obtuse and immune to factual information as possible.

"*Incroyable!*" she exclaimed with a laugh and an accent that was most decidedly French. "Oh, it is most amusing watching you try to reason with him, Dr. Watson, but it cannot be done! You see, I have always found that it is an easy thing to fool a man, but almost impossible to convince him that he has been fooled. However, I will admit that Bertie is a most exceptional case, and I must say that I find his loyalty to the Duchess of Killarney to be as endearing as it is absurd."

I turned to Bertie, anxious to see what kind of response he would have to Miss Chartier's admission that she wasn't remotely Irish, and it was like watching a baby whose favourite rattle has just disappeared beneath a piece of furniture. Not only is the rattle gone, the baby clearly wonders if the rattle ever existed in the first place now that it is no longer visible. With Miss Chartier no longer affecting her Irish brogue or capering about the room doing an Irish jig, Bertie looked at her as if he had never seen her before.

"I say, that's a French accent..." he managed.

"Yes, yes it is!" agreed Miss Chartier. "And do you know why? Because I am from Switzerland and I speak French! And look...!" She reached beneath her dress and pulled out a French derringer from the holster strapped to her leg. "A French gun! With French bullets! And when I pull the trigger it will make a French bang and the bullet will go straight through your thick English head!"

She pointed the gun at Bertie, who was now frozen into immobility, the universe as he had known it apparently ceasing to exist. By all rights, of course, I should have leapt into action to stop a paid assassin from murdering the Prince of Wales, but in the heat of the moment, and considering all that had previously occurred, as well as the thundering stupidity of the heir to the British Crown, all I could manage was a look of profound gratitude at Miss Chartier.

"Thank you! Thank you!" I then turned to Bertie. "There! What do you have to say now? Or does she need to put a bullet through your brain before you understand?"

Finally, there was a reaction from Bertie; namely, his mouth was moving, although no sounds were coming forth. Incapable of coherent speech of any kind, Bertie flung his napkin vaguely in Miss Chartier's direction, got to his feet, then tottered in ungainly fashion towards our door to make his escape.

I was relieved to see that rather than chasing him down or putting a bullet through his retreating back, Miss Chartier simply raised her eyes to the ceiling.

"I would not do that if I were you."

Something in her tone made Bertie stop in his tracks and look back at her, and she continued, "It is possible I may have an associate or two in the empty house across the street, with orders to blow the head off the next person who exits the front door...unless I give a prearranged signal from this window."

"Oh my God..." Bertie rushed to the side of the window and peeked out into the street. "They're out there waiting for me..."

"There is no point in looking for them," Miss Chartier quietly assured him. "They are well trained in the fine art of concealment, and follow the seven basic rules of all experienced assassins."

In spite of the gravity of the situation, I found myself instantly intrigued by these "seven rules" that Miss Chartier had just mentioned, and so I brought out my notebook.

"I'm sorry to interrupt," I began, "but what are those rules, exactly?"

Miss Chartier turned to me, "They are precisely what you would expect, Dr. Watson. The key to being an efficient assassin is patience; that is, taking up a position and then avoiding detection until your target is within range. And so you must be aware of the seven s's, as they are called: shape, shine, shadow, surface, silhouette, spacing, and sudden movement."

As my pencil flew over the paper, I reflected, and not for the first time, on the amazing material that Miss Chartier provided on a consistent basis, and wondered where on earth she had come by that information. Bertie had turned from the window and was staring at Miss Chartier in disbelief. Perhaps feeling a shred of sympathy for him, she offered the only meagre comfort that she could.

"If it is any consolation, Your Royal Highness, they are expert shots, and you won't even hear the bullet that kills you."

Bertie was now almost in tears. "But you were so nice to me! You brought me chicken! How can you kill someone after you bring them chicken?"

With Bertie threatening to dissolve into pure hysteria, Holmes took him by the arm and led him to the divan. "Do try to calm yourself, Bertie. Pray, take a seat, and let us see if we can contrive some way to get you out of here alive."

With Bertie seated, Holmes turned to Miss Chartier. "I take it you have all the exits covered?"

"But of course."

Holmes inclined his head in a bow towards her. "Masterfully orchestrated, Miss Chartier. Truly, a magnificent work of criminal art."

Once upon a time, a remark like that from Holmes would have caused me to panic due to the simple fact that I had only a vague idea to what he was referring. While he was apparently able to see a logical chain of facts leading to an inevitable conclusion, I was invariably able to see only the beginning and make a rough guess as to what the end might be, with everything in between a bit hazy. However, time and experience had taught me not to chastise myself too much over my own deficiencies and to simply ask Holmes to explain.

This served two functions—it filled in the blanks for the story I would later write, and it gave Holmes a chance to show off, which he enjoyed immensely. In this case, I knew that Miss Chartier had conceived of a monumental crime of some sort, because she had told me as much upon her first visit. However, at this point it didn't seem that any crime had actually been committed, aside from putting a bit of a scare into Bertie. So then, from my perspective, the criminal masterpiece alluded to by Holmes was still a blank canvas as far as I could see. Therefore, with my notebook and pencil at the ready, I prepared myself to be enlightened.

"If you could just catch me up a moment, Holmes, that would be lovely. I seem to have lost the thread somewhere."

"Isn't it obvious?" returned Holmes, knowing full well it wasn't obvious or I would never have asked for an explanation in the first place. "Miss Chartier has embarked upon an ambitious scheme that depends almost entirely on the weakness of men. In the case of Bertie and Escoffier it took no more than a fluttering eyelash and a well-turned ankle to put them entirely under her spell. As for you, my dear Watson, you were a more difficult nut to crack, but she sang you the siren song of a good story and you succumbed to her charms."

"Well, I wouldn't say that I succumbed as such, I was just...it is a good story."

"Quite."

This exchange in particular served to highlight the major difference between Holmes and myself. For him, each case was a kind of equation to be solved, with each variable plugged into the formula to lead to an irrefutable and logical result. This was all very well and good from his perspective, but then, he wasn't the one writing up the stories for publication in "The Strand." I needed a bit more than this clue, plus this motive, equals that criminal.

In addition to the bare outline of the story, I needed compelling characters, sudden revelations, and snatches of memorable dialogue. As Miss Chartier was admirably suited to provide all three of those, I quite naturally was a bit more sympathetic to her cause than Holmes might have been, although I certainly didn't want to see Bertie murdered in cold blood. As it happened, the same thought was on Bertie's mind as well, as he tugged plaintively on Holmes' sleeve.

"Mr. Holmes, please, I don't want to be assassinated!"

"A reasonable enough request," agreed Holmes. "You see, of course, how Miss Chartier has arranged affairs."

"I can't say that I do." If nothing else, Bertie was candid about his cluelessness. "As a class, we in the nobility do not much care for brains."

"I see." Holmes moved to the mantel to refill his cherry-wood pipe, lightly tamping down the tobacco, and then lighting it as he spoke. "Well, while you may have killed thousands of animals during your various safaris and expeditions, I suspect that this is the first time you have ever been in the presence of a genuine hunter, for that is what Miss Chartier is—an apex predator. Once she set her sights on you, the first task at hand was to flush her prey. She needed to get you away from your guards and well-protected estates. So, in the guise of the Duchess of Killarney, she played on your suspicions and fears regarding your advisors, then told you to consult me.

"She also involved Escoffier in her plan as not only someone you know and trust, but someone who would keep you fed in the style to which you are accustomed to lower your guard even further. She then assigned Watson the role of the respectable and trustworthy Englishman. Ultimately, you would come here of your own volition, and you would come anonymously, so at this moment no one has any idea where you are and you cannot be rescued. Still trusting her, you would have nothing to fear until the trap was well and truly sprung, at which point you would be helpless and utterly at her mercy."

"Wonderful!" I looked up to see who had said that, and was more than a little discomfited to realise that it had been me as I scribbled down Holmes' deductions word for word. "I mean terrible," I corrected myself. "Very terrible indeed."

Looking at Bertie to see how he was taking all this, I was surprised to observe an almost peaceful expression on his face.

"I understand," he said. "Well, that's that then. My mother will be pleased, at any rate."

Rising from the divan, Bertie moved to the sideboard and poured himself a large brandy, just as I observed Miss Adler reentering the room. Momentarily distracted, I wasn't sure that I had heard Bertie correctly.

"By your assassination?" I asked.

"Absolutely," answered Bertie with a nod of his head. "Miss Adler's rather colourful tirade? Comparatively mild compared to the things my own mother has said to me over the years."

"Surely you're exaggerating," I said.

"I wish I were." Bertie gave a heartfelt sigh. "From the moment I was born my mother thought I was an ugly halfwit and her opinion has not changed one jot over the years. She couldn't be bothered to nurse me, you know. Instead, I was foisted off on a wet-nurse who had six children of her own, up until the day she went mad and murdered the lot of them. As a child, I had a clever older sister my parents adored, no friends, and was regularly whipped by my tutors. I had no boyhood to speak of and gradually came to realise that what my mother really wanted was to be my father's only child.

"Oh, and my father Albert's premature death at the age of forty-two? Totally my fault, at least according to my mother. When I was nineteen years old, I had taken up with an Irish actress by the name of Nellie Clifden, and my parents were horrified at the thought of scandal and blackmail, so although my father was feeling quite ill, he travelled up to Cambridge and took me for a long walk in the rain to lecture me on my behaviour. He died three weeks later. That's why I'm called

Bertie, by the way, because I'm not worthy of the name Albert and my mother definitely doesn't think I am worthy of becoming King."

Bertie drained his snifter and proceeded to refill it, warming to his subject matter. "What the public doesn't know is that their beloved Queen Victoria is a bit of a nutter. She's been in mourning for forty years, wears the same widow's weeds every day, keeps Balmoral Castle at a brisk sixty degrees, no smoking, thirty-minute meals, and she uses cut up newspaper for toilet paper. That is the revered Queen of England for you."

Bertie turned his gaze to the portrait of Queen Victoria on our wall. "And of course, in almost every room I enter throughout the land, there's the old bird herself, staring down at me. I do recognise that I have not led an exemplary life, but just try to imagine an existence in which every room you enter has a portrait of your mother."

"Good God...you poor man," I said.

"That does explain a lot," agreed Miss Adler.

It was at that precise moment that I began to regard Bertie in a new light. Certainly the lurid details provided in Holmes' Index had cast Bertie in the darkest and most unflattering manner, and there could be no excusing his brutal behaviour to the women he used and then cast aside as so much debris. Had he been a better man he would have conscientiously conducted himself in a much more high-minded fashion.

Ignoring the privileges of his class and position, he would have been immune to the perpetual temptations thrown his way by the courtiers who surrounded him and the various women who curried his favour for what they imagined would be their own benefit, whether it be gifts, money, or simply being allowed to mingle and be seen with a certain class of people.

But the simple fact was that Bertie was not a great or even a good man. He was resoundingly, thoroughly, and pathetically average, a condition that had been immediately apparent to both his mother and father practically from the moment he was born. They had tried to mold and shape him into a person more to their liking through the right schools, the right teachers, and the right experiences, but as the years passed, all of his parents' hopes and dreams had failed at every turn. Bertie was simply Bertie. Nothing more and nothing less, and he was well aware of where he stood in the eyes of his parents.

And so, once he came of age, he fled England whenever the opportunity presented itself, to shoot practically every living creature that moved and to make the very personal acquaintance of as many courtesans as possible. And yet, hearing him speak so candidly about his life and upbringing, I began to suspect that he would quite happily have given up his exalted position for nothing more than a kind and loving word from either his mother or his late father.

Now, brandy in hand, he approached Miss Chartier, who held her gun at the ready by her side. In spite of the dire circumstances, it seemed as if a terrible weight had been lifted from Bertie. Soon enough, this half-life of perpetual adolescence, waiting in the shadows for his mother to die, would be over. He would beat her to it, and he would finally be free of the stifling and claustrophobic atmosphere he had been choking on since the day he was born.

"So then," he concluded, "I see no point in making a fuss about the inevitable. Please allow me to offer my sincere congratulations on your most successful plot."

Raising his glass in a toast to Miss Chartier, he proceeded to empty it, then set it aside. "I won't argue that the vast majority of my life has been an embarrassing abomination, so I will try to muster up a shred or two of dignity in leaving it."

Wincing a little from the stiffness in his joints, he managed to kneel before Miss Chartier, and then gazed up at her. "And surely there are worse fates than gazing into the eyes of a beautiful woman just before she blows your brains out." At this, Bertie closed his eyes and spread his arms wide. "I am ready."

Witnessing this transformation of Bertie had a mesmerising effect on everyone in the room. With the Prince of Wales kneeling in acquiescence before the daughter of Professor Moriarty, completely at her mercy, it was like watching one of Shakespeare's tragic heroes finally accepting his fate. I glanced at Holmes, expecting him to spring into action at any moment to save the life of His Royal Highness, but instead saw that he was only gazing thoughtfully at the scene, the way a fine art connoisseur might appraise a Botticelli or Holbein at the National Gallery.

Something was clearly amiss, but before I had an opportunity to discover what it might be, I was startled by a sharp noise that sounded exactly like a gunshot. Bertie immediately collapsed to the floor, but with no explosion of blood or brains. It was at that precise moment that I heard the voice of Escoffier shouting out, "Champagne!!!"

Whirling to my left, sure enough, there was Chef Escoffier, who had just entered the room and popped the cork on a bottle of Veuve Clicquot, which had produced the gunshot-like sound we all heard. Heedless of the dramatic scene that he had just interrupted, Escoffier took a few more steps into the room before seeing the inert form of Bertie on the floor.

"Dessert will be a few minutes yet and—*Mon Dieu!* What has happened to His Royal Highness?"

"He thinks he's dead," observed Miss Adler drily.

"Is he?"

"No. Just a little overwrought, I'm afraid."

Anxious for something to do, I thought I might as well try to bring Bertie round to consciousness again, and indicated as much to Holmes. "I'll get my bag."

"Hold that thought, Watson," said Holmes. "For a moment there, Bertie actually seemed vaguely noble, and almost everyone, from babies to the elderly are more tolerable when they are unconscious. Let him rest a moment while we have a quick word with Monsieur Escoffier regarding how he came to be entangled in this sorry affair."

Still holding the bottle of champagne, Escoffier gave a nervous smile. "If you don't mind, I prefer not to say. Miss Chartier...she has a gun."

"Don't worry yourself," soothed Holmes. "Miss Chartier may be evil incarnate, but she is not uncivilised. She will hardly shoot you before champagne is served. Speaking of which, some glasses would be lovely."

So that was it, the reason for Holmes' inaction as Bertie knelt before Miss Chartier awaiting his execution. Caught up in the moment, I had genuinely feared for Bertie's life, but Holmes had kept the bigger picture in mind and quite correctly deduced that if Miss Chartier had wanted to kill the Prince of Wales, he would already be dead. The fact that he was still breathing was all the evidence needed to make it abundantly clear that she had bigger plans for him. In the end, she might still assassinate him, but only after she had achieved her aim, the object of which was still unclear to me.

Miss Adler and I swiftly gathered up five champagne glasses and Escoffier filled them one by one, quite clearly relieved to be more in his element.

"I do like to start my day with a glass of champagne," Escoffier remarked. "I like to end it with champagne too. To be honest, I like a glass or two in between as well."

"Fascinating," said Holmes as I handed him a glass of champagne. "Do go on."

"I don't really know what I can tell you, Mr. Holmes."

"Then let's start with this, Monsieur Escoffier. Describe to me your greatest fear."

Escoffier's brow furrowed, giving Holmes' question serious thought. A moment later his expression brightened as the answer came to him. "That I will never fully understand tomatoes."

"Ah," Holmes was a bit bemused by Escoffier's response. "Interesting, but I was actually thinking of the accusations contained in the threatening letter you received at The Savoy Hotel."

Pulling the letter from his pocket, Holmes began reciting its salient points. "According to your anonymous correspondent, simply identified as 'One Who Knows,' you order food and wine for the restaurant and then have it delivered to your house and also the home of César Ritz. You also insist on a five percent commission paid directly to you in cash from all of The Savoy Hotel's purveyors. Finally, you offer free meals to potential investors in the hotel you and Ritz propose to open in Paris. Any truth to these allegations?"

Escoffier made a dismissive sound. "I am not a bookkeeper, Mr. Holmes. I am a chef. And who does The Savoy owe its reputation to? Me! What do a few groceries matter, and why should I not wet my beak a little?"

"Good God, man," I expostulated, "because it's a crime! You are blatantly stealing from your employer!"

"Indeed he is," agreed Miss Adler. "However, as is quite evident, the criminal acts themselves don't bother Monsieur Escoffier one bit. On the other hand, the threat of exposure and scandal put him entirely within the power of whoever wrote that letter and the letter that Bertie received. Of course, that could be none other than the industrious Miss Chartier. In Chef Escoffier's efforts to impress and seduce her, he no doubt revealed more about his future plans with Ritz than was entirely wise."

"What can I say?" replied Escoffier. "Burgundy makes you think of silly things, Bordeaux makes you talk about them, and champagne makes you do them."

"And so, thanks to a bottle or two of Veuve Clicquot, Miss Chartier knew precisely where and how hard to push to achieve her aim, which was nothing less than your complete cooperation and silence in regard to her plans for the Prince of Wales."

"She gave me no choice!" answered Escoffier. "Ritz and I, you have no idea of our plans for our hotel in Paris. It will be the grandest, most wonderful hotel the world has ever seen! Every room, every colour, every drapery and piece of furniture will be meticulously crafted and selected for the delight and comfort of our guests. I am personally designing not only our kitchen, but our dishes and silverware as well. I have already been in contact with the finest fishmongers, the most revered cheesemakers and vineyards to guarantee our guests the most exquisite gourmet meals of their lives. But this, all this, all of our hopes and dreams...we would be ruined if she exposed us!"

At this, a soft moan from Bertie indicated that he was regaining consciousness. He opened his eyes and looked around in bewilderment.

"Am I dead? Is this what heaven looks like? The room you died in?"

"No, you are not quite dead yet," answered Holmes. "A toast to the resurrection of His Royal Highness!"

As we all drank to Bertie's health, I observed that Miss Chartier still had her small gun in her hand, clearly prepared to dictate affairs as she saw fit. It was then, out of the corner of my eye, that I saw Holmes moving surreptitiously towards our sideboard, but before I could ascertain his intention, my attention was drawn by Bertie addressing Miss Chartier.

"I don't understand. Why haven't you killed me?"

"Because, my dear Bertie, while it is true that my Anarchist friends outside will pay me ten thousand pounds if you do not leave this room alive—" began Miss Chartier, only to be cut short by Holmes.

"I'm sorry to interrupt, but please be so kind as to drop your weapon, Miss Chartier."

We all turned to see Holmes, even Bertie. Still on the floor, he scuttled around like a crab to observe Holmes pointing his Webley British Bulldog at Miss Chartier, who merely raised an eyebrow in mild annoyance.

"Do you mind? I am having a private conversation with Bertie."

"Nevertheless, I must insist," replied Holmes as he cocked the Webley.

"Well, I would, but in my experience, Mr. Holmes, threats made with a gun are infinitely more convincing if the gun actually has bullets in it."

This gave Holmes pause, and I must say it gave me pause as well, as I rapidly attempted to recall all the events of the day. I had only gotten as far as Escoffier's dramatic arrival in our rooms when my train of thought was interrupted by Holmes.

"Watson?"

"Yes, Holmes?"

"When Miss Chartier was here earlier enjoying a glass or two of sherry with you, did you happen to show her where this gun was?"

Now it was all coming back to me in an unpleasant rush. "I believe I did, yes."

"And did you allow her to handle the gun?"

"I'm afraid so."

As I held my breath, Holmes opened the Webley up, looked inside, then closed it again.

"Well, that's a spirit breaker," Holmes calmly remarked, before putting the gun back in the drawer. Clearly, it was devoid of bullets, and the purpose of Miss Chartier's little charade of taking the gun from the drawer, handing it to me, then putting it back in the drawer became clear. Somewhere in all that she had contrived to empty the gun without my knowledge, and I reflected once again upon the fact that she was truly a criminal artist through and through. Holmes seemed to appreciate this as well, for instead of upbraiding me for my stupidity, he simply turned to her and said, "Do carry on."

"Thank you. But first..." Miss Chartier directed her glance at Escoffier, "...Auguste, don't you have something in the oven?"

"Yes! Of course! I shall be but a moment!"

As Escoffier hurried to our door and exited, Miss Chartier returned her attention to the still prone Bertie. "As I was saying, ten thousand pounds to kill you is a generous amount, but you are the Prince of Wales, a man with considerable resources at your disposal. I thought perhaps you would like to make me a counteroffer."

"You mean..." I could almost see the long disused gears of Bertie's brain struggling to turn. "...I could pay you not to kill me?"

"What a clever Prince you are," returned Miss Chartier with a smile. "Yes."

Bertie struggled to his feet. "Well, of course! I'll double it! Twenty thousand pounds!"

"You can do better than that."

"I don't know that I can, quite honestly. I've already used up most of my allowance for the year, and if I ask Mother for more money she'll be quite cross with me."

"Think, Bertie," encouraged Miss Chartier.

As painful a process as this was, Bertie set himself to the unfamiliar task, his face contorting like a gargoyle's under the strain until finally, a new light appeared in his eyes. "Oh, of course! Baron Rothschild! I'll ask him! He's always good for a few pounds when I'm a bit short."

"Ah yes," interjected Miss Adler, "whenever the monarchy is in trouble, they run to the bankers, who in turn demand their own favours from the government so that the rich, as always, get richer. Honestly, could the royal family be any more pathetic and ridiculous?"

"I say," I responded, feeling the tug of patriotism upon me, "the monarchy may not be everyone's cup of tea, but is democracy any better? It's nothing more or less than mob rule. I mean, look at America! You can have a kind, decent, wise President one moment, and then an insufferably incompetent fool in office the very next day."

"You're thinking of Abraham Lincoln and his successor Andrew Johnson, of course," noted Holmes.

"Of course!"

"Well, unless I'm greatly mistaken," Miss Adler continued, "Baron Rothschild, despite his considerable resources, is of no use to Bertie. He does not have what Miss Chartier wants."

Bertie turned to Miss Chartier. "Then for God's sake, what do you want?"

As all eyes turned to her, I fancied this was a scene that she had played out in her mind many times from the moment she had begun plotting this particular crime. It was a crime as complex and inspired as it was audacious, and bearing that in mind it was essential that she should have the right audience before her to fully appreciate every facet of her criminal genius.

"What do I want, Your Royal Highness?" she began. "I am so glad that you asked. But do not needlessly fret yourself regarding anything so vulgar as money. There is only one thing that I desire from you—the Koh-i-Noor Diamond."

Chapter Seven
Of Diamonds and Soufflés

And with that, the object of Miss Chartier's bold game came fully into the light. Of course, in her efforts to pique my interest upon her first visit, she had suggested as much by her emphasis on Queen Victoria's Diamond Jubilee. These were mere crumbs thrown upon the trail for me to follow, and follow them I had, even to the point of asking Bertie if his mother happened to own any significant diamonds. Now, having Bertie precisely where she wanted him, there was no longer any need to rely on hints and veiled meaning, as she was ready to claim her prize. From Bertie's perspective, however, she may as well have asked him to bring down the moon from the night sky and put it in her pocket.

"What? The Koh-i-Noor Diamond? What are you talking about? That's impossible! You have no idea what that diamond is worth!"

"Actually, I know exactly what it is worth," answered Miss Chartier. "Two million pounds. That is the amount that a buyer in India has offered to pay."

Not being overly familiar with the market for precious stones, I had no idea that any gem could fetch such an astronomical price and said as much. "Great Heavens above! That's a fortune! You would be one of the richest women in the world!"

"If you will recall," pointed out Miss Chartier, "I believe I did say that I might profit slightly from the game."

This was quite true, although I must say that Miss Chartier's idea of a slight profit diverged significantly from my own. As for Bertie, judging by the manner in which he was lifting his chin and thrusting his chest out, he was grateful for the opportunity to assert his authority and to put Miss Chartier firmly in her place.

"Yes, well, I am very sorry to tell you, Miss Chartier, that this entire enterprise of yours has been completely pointless! The Koh-i-Noor is under lock and key! Beyond that, it's in a castle! A castle protected by guards who have guns! In other words, and I can't possibly state this any more clearly, the Koh-i-Noor Diamond is completely and utterly beyond your grasp! You may threaten me all you like, but you will never get your hands on it!"

It was an impressive little speech, and would have most likely put an end to any designs that Miss Chartier had on the Koh-i-Noor Diamond, save for the fact that at the end of Bertie's lecture on the Crown's security measures, she proceeded to pull the Koh-i-Noor Diamond itself from her bodice. Approximately the size of a plum, she held it up by its chain and it shimmered and danced with fire in the light as we all stared in disbelief and Miss Chartier regarded Bertie with a bemused expression.

"You were saying?"

"Oh my God...how..." Bertie was quite literally staggered by the appearance of the diamond, reaching for the divan in an effort to steady himself. "She has the Koh-i-Noor..."

Miss Chartier, on the other hand, was entirely in her element. Calm and collected, with her scheme unfolding like clockwork, she held the gem up by its chain, turning it this way and that to drink in every perfect facet of its beauty.

"It is a pretty little thing, is it not? And like so many pretty little things it comes with a dark and violent history."

The gem itself, in all of its magnificence, was one thing, but it was this history just alluded to by Miss Chartier that really

119

caught my attention. Pulling out my notebook and pencil, I determined to learn as much as I could about the Koh-i-Noor before there was consternation regarding possession of the diamond, which I was quite sure was in the offing.

"Really? Do you happen to have details that you'd care to share regarding the gem's history, Miss Chartier? The darker and more violent, the better."

"Of course. Anything for you, Dr. Watson. The Koh-i-Noor originally came from India. Exactly when and where, no one knows, but it was in the possession of Babur, the founder of the Mughal Empire in 1526. After he died, possibly from poisoning, it was placed in the Peacock Throne of Shah Jahan, who was subsequently arrested by his own son and declared incompetent to rule. It then made its way to the Persian Nader Shah, who was the wealthiest man on earth and known for being particularly cruel and violent. He ordered mass killings of his enemies and had their skulls heaped in piles outside his palace.

"When he suspected his own son of plotting against him, he ordered the boy blinded, with his eyes brought to Nader Shah on a plate. One night, as he lay sleeping, he was set upon by no fewer than fifteen assassins, and his head was severed clean from his body. At the conclusion of the Second Anglo-Sikh War, the diamond was ceded as a spoil of war to Queen Victoria herself, who has owned it for the past forty-eight years...up until today."

"And is it really that valuable?" I asked, quite certain that she was exaggerating its worth for effect.

"It was once said," continued Miss Chartier, "that if a powerful man should throw five stones, one east, one west, one north, one south, and one as high as possible into the sky, that if you filled the air between those points with solid gold, it would not equal the value of the Koh-i-Noor. It is the ultimate spoil of war with a bloody trail from one owner to the next, and it even comes with its very own curse—'He who owns this diamond will own the world, but will also know all its misfortunes. Only God, or a woman, can wear it with impunity.'"

She favoured us all with a smile before putting the chain around her neck and allowing the diamond to sparkle against the green fabric of her dress. "It suits me, don't you think?"

Bertie had managed to seat himself on the divan, taking all of this in with an expression of utter disbelief.

"But how..." he began falteringly.

"...did I happen to acquire it?" Miss Chartier thoughtfully finished his sentence for him. "I have Your Royal Highness to thank for that."

"That's not true!" Bertie objected. "Preposterous! I would never agree to such a thing!"

"I never said you agreed to it, but one week ago, you were gracious enough to give the Duchess of Killarney your autograph. An autograph that happened to be at the bottom of a personal request from you to have the Koh-i-Noor Diamond removed for cleaning in preparation for the Queen wearing it during the Diamond Jubilee. When it comes to crime, I follow the motto of our friend Escoffier, 'Keep it simple.'"

True to form, faced with the evidence that he had basically handed over an almost priceless diamond to a master criminal, the first thing that popped into Bertie's mind was getting into trouble with his mother. He was forever the naughty schoolboy, not the middle-aged Prince of Wales who had allowed his libidinous urges to lead him into being duped by a beautiful woman. "My God...when the Queen realises it's missing..."

"She won't," replied Miss Chartier.

"Why not?" asked Bertie.

"Because the Koh-i-Noor was returned three days later."

"What?" Bertie was completely at sea. "I don't understand."

"I believe that what Miss Chartier is saying," explained Miss Adler, "is that a replica of the Koh-i-Noor was created and returned to Queen Victoria at Balmoral Castle."

"Just so," confirmed Miss Chartier. "The Queen is old, with poor eyesight. It will never occur to her that it is a fake, and no one else will look at it closely enough to know the difference. And even if they did, who would dare tell her?"

During all this, I had been feverishly writing down every detail and word that I could, but at this final revelation I couldn't stop myself from bursting out, "My God, it's the perfect crime! Bravo!"

"I say, Dr. Watson!" objected Bertie. "Whose side are you on?"

"I must apologise for my colleague," answered Holmes. "With a few exceptions, his allegiance is to whatever happens to make the best story."

"And I do wish that were the end of the story," said Miss Chartier. "Really and truly. However, the world is changing, and even we criminals must move with the times."

It was only at that moment that I fully apprehended the absurdity of the situation. Miss Chartier had successfully stolen the Koh-i-Noor Diamond and quite literally had it hanging around her neck. Why on earth was she wearing it in the rooms of Sherlock Holmes and not already halfway to India to collect her two million pounds? Similarly befuddled, Bertie summarised the situation perfectly.

"You have the diamond! What else do you want?"

"An excellent question," responded Miss Chartier, "with a very simple answer. My buyer fancies himself a modern man, and he has conditions. To his credit, he is a patriotic Indian Maharajah. He wants the stone returned to the land of its origin. But that is not enough. He wants proof of ownership, provenance, and so on. So yes, I have the Koh-i-Noor itself, and I also have this..." Reaching beneath her dress and into her boot, she pulled out a photograph, "...a lovely portrait of Bertie and I together."

Caught up in the drama of the situation, and cognisant of the fact that she had only recently produced a gun from beneath her dress, I heard myself saying, "Good Lord, what else do you have under that dress?" Instantly aware of everyone in the room staring at me, I tried to backtrack as quickly as I could manage, weakly muttering, "I didn't mean that."

Delighted with my embarrassment and discomfort, Miss Chartier proceeded to hike her dress up above her knee. "No, no. I would be delighted to show you everything beneath my dress, Dr. Watson..."

I like to think that I would have done the gentlemanly thing and averted my eyes had she revealed the white rotundities of her callipygian charms, or chosen to unveil the Gates of Venus, as the esteemed Benjamin Franklin once put it upon a visit to France, but to my simultaneous relief and disappointment, she did nothing of the kind. Instead, she reached into the top of her stocking and removed some folded papers.

"...and now all I need is this legal document signed, officially transferring ownership of the Koh-i-Noor to me, so that I may pass it on to the Maharajah and collect my fee. I might add that he has graciously agreed not to reveal the details of our arrangement to spare the Queen any embarrassment. As her son and heir, your signature is all that I require, Your Royal Highness." Putting the document on the table, she turned to me. "Have you a pen, Dr. Watson? I need it signed in triplicate."

"What is the world coming to?" remarked Miss Adler. "The greatest criminal mind of the century now needs to be a lawyer?"

"Well, these days, what is the difference?" returned Miss Chartier, as I put a pen and inkpot on the table as she requested.

"So, that's what you need?" asked Bertie. "My signature? This is the last piece of the puzzle in your grandiose scheme, me signing these documents?"

"If you would be so kind," answered Miss Chartier.

"And what if I don't? What if I choose to just sit here and not leave these rooms? What then? Why should I sign?"

With that, Miss Chartier pointed her gun at Bertie's forehead and cocked it. "Because I am asking nicely."

"And so am I." I turned to see that Miss Adler had somehow produced a gun of her own, and was pointing it directly at Miss Chartier. "Kindly hand your weapon to Dr. Watson, Miss Chartier."

Not showing the least alarm, Miss Chartier regarded the gun being pointed at her with little more reaction than a raised eyebrow. "Ah. Nicely played, Miss Adler. Your little trip to the bedroom gave you the opportunity to arm yourself."

"Considering the company, I thought it might prove useful."

"A most excellent inclination, my dear," agreed Holmes.

Showing every courtesy, Miss Chartier uncocked her gun, then offered it to me on her open palm.

"And now," Miss Adler continued, "to conclude this sordid affair, please return the Koh-i-Noor Diamond to His Royal Highness."

Reaching behind her neck to unclasp the necklace, Miss Chartier proceeded to hand the massive diamond over to an ecstatic Bertie.

"Excellent! And that is that, Miss Chartier! I shall personally see to it that you become well acquainted with the inside of Brixton Women's Prison. In fact, I shall escort you there myself! Consider yourself outwitted by Sherlock Holmes!"

"Excuse me?" objected Miss Adler.

"And his assistant, of course!"

"Stop talking, or I'll shoot you myself."

"We must celebrate!" Bertie enthused. "Do you know what we need?"

In answer to that question, our door burst open and Escoffier entered bearing a tray with a covered dish and a large cloth napkin.

"Soufflé is here!!!"

Bertie was absolutely beside himself with delight. Caught up in the moment, everything was going wonderfully for him. He was no longer looking down the barrel of a gun, the Koh-i-Noor Diamond was nestling comfortably in his pocket, and the greatest chef in the world had just arrived with one of his most famous dishes. Bertie clapped his hands enthusiastically, practically dancing in place.

"Bravo, Auguste! And most excellent timing! A celebration is in order! Bring it here, my good man!"

Personally, I was much less enthused than Bertie, as I remembered not only the threat of Anarchist assassins outside of our rooms, but the much more immediate and tangible threat of Miss Chartier inside our rooms. While we may have been successful in disarming her and taking possession of the diamond, that did not mean she was incapable of more mischief.

Sure enough, as Escoffier approached Bertie with the tray holding the soufflé, Miss Chartier snatched it out of his hands and was at the open window in a heartbeat. To Bertie's horror, she held the tray outside the window as he moved towards her.

"Ah, ah, ah!" she warned. "One more step and the soufflé goes into the street to feed the dogs."

"You monster! You wouldn't!"

"Wouldn't I?" Miss Chartier pretended to lose her grip on the tray, eliciting a cry of pure despair from Bertie.

"Stop! For the love of God! Mr. Holmes, do something!"

"Do what? It's only a soufflé."

"Only a soufflé?" Bertie couldn't believe his ears. "What kind of savage are you? It's a soufflé created by Auguste Escoffier!"

"Thank you!" chimed in Escoffier.

With the needs of his belly clearly overriding any other considerations, Bertie dropped to his knees and began shuffling slowly towards Miss Chartier in supplication. "Miss Chartier, please don't do anything rash. Perhaps we can reach an understanding."

"Such as?"

"What do you want?"

"Well, to begin with, I feel quite certain that the inside of Brixton Prison would not agree with me."

"Very well," replied Bertie. "I promise that no charges will be brought against you. But in return, you must signal your accomplices across the street to leave and then hand over the soufflé."

"Agreed."

Balancing the tray on the ledge of the window, Miss Chartier pulled a white handkerchief from her sleeve and waved it vigourously up and down. She then turned to offer the tray to Bertie, who eagerly grabbed it by both handles. As he did so, Miss Chartier reached beneath the napkin on the tray and to my astonishment, pulled out an iron manacle. Faster than thought, she secured the manacle around Bertie's wrist, and I could see that it was attached by a chain to one of the tray's handles. It had all happened in a heartbeat, and Bertie looked down at his chained wrist in bewilderment.

"Good God woman, what have you done?"

"I would say," began Holmes, "that she has quite neatly trapped her rather foolish and overconfident prey."

With all thoughts of a warm and tasty soufflé dashed from his mind, Bertie stared in horror at the covered dish on the tray.

"What is it? What's under this lid?"

"You're a big, brave, bold Prince, aren't you?" taunted Miss Chartier. "Lift it up and see for yourself."

"If you value your life, don't touch it!" cried Holmes.

"Oh, what could it be?" continued Miss Chartier, slowly making a tour of our rooms and clearly enjoying the moment. "I am a criminal genius, after all. Perhaps it is some kind of venomous creature...do you like snakes, Your Royal Highness?"

"No! I positively loathe snakes!" Beads of sweat were now clearly visible on Bertie's brow.

Scanning our bookshelves, Miss Chartier took hold of the blowpipe that little Tonga, the murderous Andaman Islander, had used to shoot poison darts at Holmes and I at the conclusion of "The Sign of the Four." Showing a flattering familiarity with my work, Miss Chartier proceeded to reference that very story.

"Or possibly it is a dart tipped with a poison from the Andaman Islands. It will shoot out once the lid is removed, pierce your neck, and you will die choking on your own blood."

At this, Miss Chartier favoured me with a quick wink, and I was once again reminded of her almost inhuman degree of self-possession. But then it occurred to me that despite the tension of the situation, she was once again giving me wonderful material, and she was well aware of that fact. I resolved to thank her at some suitable moment, if in fact there would ever be a suitable moment. Enjoying her power over Bertie, she placed the blowpipe to her lips and watched Bertie cower before her.

"No, please!"

"Or perhaps..." Miss Chartier now sauntered towards Bertie with a nonchalant air, "...it is even more terrifying than you can imagine. Perhaps it is..." She pulled the cloche from the dish with a sudden motion as Bertie screamed in terror, "...a soufflé!"

Sure enough, a large, beautiful soufflé was on the platter, although to my untrained eye it appeared somewhat lopsided in appearance.

"Nicely done, Auguste," remarked Miss Chartier. "It looks most delicious."

After having the soufflé snatched away from him, I had almost forgotten that Escoffier was still in the room. He nodded nervously at Miss Chartier's praise.

"*Merci beaucoup.* I followed your instructions *exactement.*"

"But look, it's fallen!" cried Bertie. "It's not a proper soufflé! There's something wrong with it!"

"I do apologise, Your Royal Highness," returned Escoffier, "but it is not my doing. Miss Chartier insisted on a very special ingredient that caused the soufflé to fall, I am afraid."

"So it's poisoned! She's poisoned it! Well, I'm not eating it! Not a bite!"

"Oh dear," chided Miss Chartier, "and here I thought His Royal Highness was an adventurous eater of the very first order." She proceeded to break off a piece of the soufflé and put it into her mouth. "Mmm...well, if it is poison, it is a most delicious poison, I must say."

Seeing that Miss Chartier was clearly enjoying herself, Bertie reached for the top of the soufflé to take a piece for himself, only to be brought up short by Holmes.

"Bertie, I implore you, as you value your life, do not move a muscle."

Summoning what little willpower he had, Bertie managed to resist the urge to sample the soufflé, his hand frozen in place as Holmes retrieved his magnifying lens and proceeded to examine the soufflé from every possible angle.

"Well? What do you see, Mr. Holmes?" asked Bertie.

"It's not what I see that is the problem," answered Holmes. "It is what I hear."

With infinite care, Holmes lifted the top of the soufflé up to reveal that the soufflé itself was hollow. Inside it, there was no mistaking what was clearly a small explosive device. Crafted out of some kind of metal, I had never seen anything quite like it, and assumed it was the latest version of the Anarchists' genius for bomb making. The black and red wires sticking out of it and an audible ticking sound left no doubt in Bertie's mind as to its purpose.

"Oh my God, it's a bomb!" cried Bertie. "Get rid of it, Mr. Holmes! Throw it out the window, for God's sake!"

I could see Holmes swallow hard as he delicately took the bomb by its edges and tried to lift it off the platter, but it refused to budge.

"Easier said than done, I'm afraid," replied Holmes. "It appears to be welded to the platter itself, and with Your Royal

Highness manacled to the very same platter, if I throw it out the window, you're going with it."

"Yes, that is the point," agreed Miss Chartier. "And I must say, I found the Anarchists to be most ingenious when it comes to making bombs. This is their smallest model, designed to completely obliterate anything in a five-foot radius, but its force dissipates rapidly...although I can't swear that your windows will survive the blast. Bertie, on the other hand...someone will have to pour him into his coffin."

"Oh my God, oh my God..." Bertie was clearly descending into hysteria, and I don't know that I would have done otherwise if I found myself chained to such a fiendish device.

"Please don't move!" instructed Holmes. "The vibrations might set it off!"

"I can't help it! I'm going to be blown to pieces!"

Bertie was trembling where he stood and something had to be done. Holmes took Bertie's elbow, then looked at me and Miss Adler.

"Watson, Irene, help me get Bertie to the divan."

With all three of us concentrating our efforts, Miss Adler offered support at Bertie's back as Holmes and I lifted him by his legs and carried him over to the divan as carefully as possible. Halfway there, Bertie shot an accusing glance at Escoffier.

"How could you, Auguste?"

"It was Miss Chartier! She gave me no choice!"

Settling Bertie onto the divan, Holmes and I both kept hold of his arms to try to keep the bomb as still and level as possible.

"You have to disarm it!" ordered Bertie.

"Yes, well..." Holmes was clearly put out of sorts by Bertie's request.

"Do you know how to disarm bombs, Holmes?" I asked. "You never mentioned it to me."

"Of course he can!" Bertie insisted. "He's Sherlock Holmes! He can identify one hundred and forty different types of cigar and pipe ash! He must know how to defuse a bomb!"

"Actually, no," admitted Holmes, "although it is on my to-do list. Irene? Would you be able to offer any assistance in the matter, perchance?"

"No, I'm afraid not," answered Miss Adler. "Oddly enough, they didn't teach bomb defusing at opera school."

"*Quel dommage.*"

We all turned to see Miss Chartier observing our predicament with a mixture of amusement and contempt. "What a pity. If only there were someone in the room who grew up around her father's criminal empire. Someone who knew how to counterfeit, pick locks, and defuse bombs."

Bertie looked at her with imploring eyes. "Miss Chartier, I am begging you. Please..."

"There is no need to beg," she answered coldly. "Business is business. And this seems like a good time to reopen negotiations."

"What are you talking about?" Bertie was incredulous. "The bomb could go off at any second!"

Approaching Bertie from behind, Miss Chartier used her handkerchief to wipe his fevered brow and then thoughtfully repositioned a few strands of his wayward hair.

"No, we have a few moments. I utilised the services of Nikolai Volya, the finest bomb-maker among the Anarchists. It has been rigged to chime ten times before it explodes, which will give everyone plenty of time to clear the room...unless, of course, you happen to be chained to the bomb."

"What do you want? Anything!" pleaded Bertie.

"An excellent attitude," said Miss Chartier as she looked around the room, apparently cataloguing what would suit her needs best. "First, Miss Adler, may I trouble you for your gun?"

Having little choice in the matter, Miss Adler handed over her weapon, at which point Miss Chartier removed the bullets, then tossed the gun onto the floor before turning to me. "And Dr. Watson? My gun, please?"

As I held the gun out to her, I looked directly into her eyes, hoping to see some inkling of her intent. Was she really prepared to blow up the Prince of Wales if any one of us failed to do her bidding? As always, however, she was impossible to read, and in dealing with her it was always best to remember that she was most definitely her father's child. The moment she had her gun back in her hand, she moved closer to the traumatised Bertie, who couldn't take his eyes off the bomb sitting on his lap.

"And Bertie? I believe you have something I want."

With his free hand, Bertie pulled the Koh-i-Noor Diamond from his pocket and held it up by its chain. As ever, it sparkled and danced in the light as it had for hundreds of years across two continents, and almost always to the regret of whoever happened to possess it. In this instance, there seemed to be no reason for additional bloodshed, as Bertie merely had to comply with Miss Chartier's wishes. The Anarchists across the street had already been waved away, and once Bertie returned the diamond to Miss Chartier and signed the legal documents, she would surely disarm the bomb and exit in haste. I had no doubt she had already made travel preparations to take herself to India as quickly as possible to hand over the gem and collect her fee.

And yet, as all this flashed through my mind, Bertie hesitated, and I could see that his grip on the Koh-i-Noor was tightening.

Chapter Eight

Bertie the Hero

Bertie stared unblinkingly at the diamond in his hand, seeing in it who knew what? For his entire life he had always been deferential and submissive when it came to important decisions, whether they might be personal or public. Despite his exalted status, he was never really in charge of his own affairs, and there was almost always someone is his life, whether a parent, tutor, or advisor to order him about. As much as he might have rebelled by way of his scandalous behaviour, that was all so much the kicking and squalling of a spoiled child. Here, once again, he was being asked to be a good boy and do as he was told, but somehow a small flame of resistance seemed to have been sparked inside him.

"Mr. Holmes," he asked, his voice hoarse with emotion, "is there anything you can do to spare me this humiliation?"

"I can only advise you to give Miss Chartier the diamond and sign the documents," replied Holmes, as pragmatic as ever. "But it is entirely up to you. You are measuring the value of your life against the value of a shiny lump of carbon."

"Yes...that is the choice, isn't it? This shiny lump of carbon or my life..." Bertie twisted in his seat to gaze at the portrait of Queen Victoria on the wall. "Which one, Mother? Which one would you prefer? Which one would you love?"

Hot tears began streaming down Bertie's cheeks as the sadness and regrets of his entire life burst through the noble façade he had been forced to put on practically from the moment he was born. Who knows what difference some form of genuine love or affection would have made to his life? It was now a question beyond answering, and it was Holmes who endeavoured to return Bertie's focus to the crisis at hand.

"No, no, let's not go down that path, Bertie. Pull yourself together, for God's sake."

"I know you mean well, Mr. Holmes," returned Bertie, his bottom lip quivering, "but honestly, is my life worth anything? Everything you said about me is true. I am a royal parasite...a self-indulgent child...almost universally despised. It will only become worse once I am King."

"Perhaps you could abdicate and go to America?" offered Miss Adler.

"Don't be absurd!" scoffed Escoffier. "He would not last a week. I visited America once and found thirty-two religions and only one sauce. Barbarians..."

Glancing at Bertie, I could see a look of firm resolution forming in his countenance, as he shifted from self-pity to a kind of hopeless defiance. "No, the simple truth is this...my life isn't worth saving, but as my final act I will save the Koh-i-Noor Diamond for the Queen! I refuse to hand it over! Let it be plucked from my shattered remains!"

With that, Bertie closed his hand around the diamond and clutched it to his chest, defying anyone to try and take it away from him. This, needless to say, presented a very delicate situation for everyone in the room, save perhaps Miss Chartier. There was no doubt in my mind that she was fully prepared to allow Bertie to be torn to pieces when the device exploded, and in my mind's eye I could see her casually sifting through the carnage until she found the necklace and put it back around her neck.

On the other hand, the assassination of Bertie did not bode particularly well for anyone else in the room. Escoffier, of course, had served as an accomplice to Miss Chartier and had made the soufflé in which the bomb was hidden. As for Holmes, Miss Adler, and myself, it's reasonable to say that our consulting practice would never recover from allowing the Prince of Wales to be murdered in our rooms.

Gazing about me, I could see that Escoffier was not inclined to offer any practical assistance, and after all, he had merely made the soufflé, not the bomb itself. If it came to a court case, he could only be charged as an accessory to the crime, and there was no question that in his position at The Savoy Hotel he had any number of powerful and wealthy friends who would come to his defence. Dismissing the idea of any help from that quarter, I calculated that if Holmes and I fell upon Miss Chartier simultaneously and Miss Adler attempted to disarm her, we might very well succeed, but that would accomplish nothing of consequence, for the defiant Bertie would still be manacled to the bomb.

The situation appeared to be impossible, but just as that thought struck me, so did an impossible solution. It was only a glimmer of an idea, but I knew that I didn't have time to think it through in any kind of detail. Rather, I had to start talking and then simply make it up as I went along. In other words, I had to tell a story.

"Now, hold on!" I began, my creative faculties stirred to their peak by sheer adrenaline as I focused my attention on Bertie. "I think...and I realise I am in the minority here, but I think you could be a fine King of England!"

I was disconcertingly aware of the expressions of shock and disbelief turned my way by everyone in the room, as if I had just suggested that His Royal Highness would make a fine dolphin or tulip, but having embarked upon this unlikely and precarious path, I now had no choice but to carry it out to its logical conclusion.

"I mean what I say!" I continued. "Yes, you may appear to be a ridiculous, commonplace jackass, but people can change! And for the sake of England, sir, you must change!"

"I must?" Was that a glint of hope I saw in Bertie's eye? If all he needed was some thread to lead him out of the labyrinth he had constructed around himself and to offer the prospect that his life needn't end by being splattered all over our walls, then I was damned well going to give it to him.

"If you do not, it will mean the end of the British Monarchy and chaos and revolution in the streets! Yes, you may have spent your entire life emasculated and marginalised as the Prince of Wales. Yes, you may have been an object of mockery and derision practically from the moment you were born. And yes, you may have wasted almost your entire life on one frivolous pursuit after another. But you will have a chance to redeem yourself as King! Now, think! How will you do that?"

It seemed, in that moment, as if time had stopped. I could see Bertie thinking, or at the very least, making an effort to think, and that alone gave me hope that perhaps there would indeed be a way out of this dilemma. And then Bertie spoke.

"I don't know...perhaps I could start a war?"

I have known disappointment in my life. I have known pain, sorrow, and loss. I have been gazed upon with indifference by women I adored and watched brave soldiers pass away despite my best efforts to save their lives. But none of those experiences enveloped me with the hopelessness that I felt upon hearing Bertie's words. There was only one thing I could possibly do at this crucial juncture and so I did it, turning to the most brilliant man I have ever known for counsel and help.

"For God's sake, Holmes, help me out."

Drawing himself up to his full height, Holmes took a deep breath, then began the serious work of trying to extricate us from the abyss which threatened to engulf us.

"Well, I will say this for His Royal Highness, in his efforts to get away from his mother, he has travelled the world extensively and has always been well received in foreign lands. Indeed, he is perhaps the most cosmopolitan man of our time."

"That is quite true," added Escoffier, "and he speaks excellent French."

"*Merci, mon ami!*" Like a perpetually whipped dog, Bertie's eyes shone with gratitude at the smallest compliment or act of kindness. Seeing that, I quickly determined to shore up his damaged ego even further.

"Not to mention German..." I added.

"*Natürlich, mein vater war Deutscher!*" Bertie was positively growing before our eyes.

"Also," observed Holmes, "thanks to his fascination with military uniforms he is quite up-to-date on all the armies in Europe, and he has considerable influence in Russia and Germany because he is uncle to both the Czar and the Kaiser!"

"Yes, yes, little Nicky and Willie..." Bertie was clearly seeing his quite deranged nephews as small children in his mind's eye, before power and privilege had twisted them into the cruel and pathetic despots they had both become. I felt that we had made some progress, but we still needed one final push to get Bertie's state of mind where it needed to be. Clearly sensing the same thing, Holmes charged once more into the breach.

"But perhaps his clearest path to redemption lies not in war or actual accomplishments, but in, how shall I put it...?"

Holmes looked meaningfully at me, and it was in that moment that all of our years of friendship and the adventures we had shared came together as our minds became one.

"Tradition!!!" I fairly shouted. "Like kippers and kidneys for breakfast! Tea and crumpets! Cricket, Westminster Abbey, and the White Cliffs of Dover! The King of England and the royal family must uphold British tradition!"

"And there is your answer, sir, your path to redemption!" added Holmes. "Along with your family, becoming a beacon of bourgeois domesticity; that is, giving the British public the comforting spectacle of nicely dressed people doing nice things in nice places."

"Precisely!" I agreed. "You shall serve as the shining symbol of everything that is great about Britain to every country around the world! And all that your loyal subjects require in return is the occasional parade and a friendly wave once in a while."

"I like waving!" Bertie enthused.

"Well, of course you do!" enthused Holmes, doing his best to keep our momentum going. "And you're quite splendid at it!"

I could see that Bertie had arrived at a precipice in his own mind, but it was here that he paused, one more issue clearly weighing on him. He turned to Miss Adler, hope and trepidation in his eyes.

"And what...what does Miss Adler think?"

"What do I think?" repeated Miss Adler. "I think that Mr. Holmes and Dr. Watson have made a series of excellent arguments regarding your future prospects as the King of England. Every day represents a new opportunity to do good— to go out into the world and through kindness and generosity, improve or even transform the lives of people less fortunate than yourself. While the sins of the past cannot be erased, you can make certain that they are never repeated, and through your own actions, you can dedicate yourself to your redemption in countless different ways—supporting the arts, raising money for hospitals, offering help to the poor and indigent. However, in the end, it will all come down to one very simple question. Will you be able to keep your pants on and behave like a civilised human being?"

"Why..." Bertie's eyes darted back and forth as he considered this, the enormity of the task all too apparent to him. "I...I believe I can! Yes...Yes!!!"

Not wanting to give him any time to reconsider, I swiftly retrieved the legal papers brought by Marie Chartier, all the while determined to keep his ego well fed.

"Bravo! Then you, sir, shall be exactly like Shakespeare's Prince Hal! A dissolute, drunken, disreputable Prince, but a truly heroic King!"

"You mean I would be like the Henry the Fifth? A hero? I could be a hero?"

"Absolutely!" I put the legal papers before Bertie and thrust a pen into his hand. "So you must do your duty, give Miss Chartier the diamond, and sign these papers for God and Country!"

"Yes, why I'll be just like Henry the Fifth!" Bertie was in a rapturous state of ecstasy. "I'm going to be a hero—"

But before Bertie could get another word out, an ominous chime came from the bomb, sounding like nothing short of a death knell. Suddenly, it felt like all of the air had been sucked out of the room as Bertie screamed and shoved the Koh-i-Noor Diamond into Miss Chartier's hand. Frantically, he began signing the legal documents as another chime sounded.

Cool as ever, Miss Chartier polished the diamond on her sleeve and then turned to me, "And Dr. Watson, I will need a witness, please."

Taking the pen from Bertie as another chime sounded, it wasn't immediately apparent to me where I should sign, as Bertie had taken up most of the blank space with his large, florid signature.

"Just sign it!" Bertie fairly screamed at me as another chime sounded. "Anywhere!"

As I was about to put pen to paper, another thought struck me regarding potential legal ramifications, and I turned to Miss Chartier. "Should I include my middle name?"

"For God's sake," Bertie took hold of my wrist and dragged it towards the document. "Sign it!"

As another chime sounded, I quickly put my signature to the three pages. Bertie swiftly gathered them up and held them out to Miss Chartier. "There! You have what you want! Legal title to the Koh-i-noor Diamond! Now please disarm the bomb!"

Relishing Bertie's fear and panic, Miss Chartier held the diamond up to the light to watch it sparkle as another chime sounded.

"Oh, very well. Now, let me see if I can remember. Did Nikolai say it was a red wire or a black wire that I should pull out?" She paused, her hand hovering over the bomb as another chime sounded. "If only I wasn't an emotional woman who can't make good decisions..."

"Please, please, I'm begging you!" Bertie's face was a mask of pure panic. "As my first kingly order I will legalise women riding bicycles!"

"So many wires and colours..." Miss Chartier might as well have been picking a flower for a bouquet, her fingers reaching for a wire as another chime sounded. "It is all so confusing for my simple woman's mind..."

"That's eight!" cried Bertie.

"I don't know...maybe I should just pick my favourite colour..."

As the ninth chime sounded, Bertie closed his eyes and let loose a primal scream of terror just as Holmes darted forward and plucked out one of the black wires from the infernal device. We all stared at the bomb, waiting for the tenth chime, but the tenth chime never came, and to my indescribable relief, the ticking stopped. Bertie looked from the bomb to Holmes in disbelief.

"You've done it! Thank God! I owe you my life, Mr. Holmes!"

Holmes' calm demeanour was in stark contrast to Bertie's now ragged and disheveled appearance, as he held the black wire he had just pulled from the bomb up to the light, looking at it closely. "I'm not entirely sure that you do."

Holmes then proceeded to do the last thing that I expected, putting the black wire in his mouth, taking a bite, then chewing thoughtfully. "Liquorice," he pronounced, "and quite tasty liquorice as well."

"What?" Bertie asked. "What do you mean liquorice?"

With the ticking from the bomb having ceased, I was emboldened to approach it and ran my fingernail across the top of it, then put my finger in my mouth, which was immediately filled with a sweet taste.

"Why, it's sugar! The entire contraption is made of sugar!"

Marie Chartier turned her attention to Holmes, regarding him with thoughtful eyes. "I am most impressed. How did you know?"

"It was Watson's earlier comment about a delicious birthday candle that planted the seed in my mind," Holmes began, "and it also explained why you needed Escoffier and his particular field of expertise."

Bertie couldn't take his eyes off the "bomb," clearly seeing it in an entirely new light. Tentatively, he plucked off a red wire and tasted it.

"My God...you made this, Auguste?"

"*Mais oui!*" The smug smile on Escoffier's face was quite a thing to behold. "It is the art of pastillage, *n'est-ce pas?* A hard sugar that can be shaped and painted with food colouring to create any object you desire. I simply concealed a small clock and a bell inside for the sounds."

Escoffier turned to Miss Chartier, hope and fear in his eyes. "So, I have done as you asked?"

"Beautifully, Auguste."

"Then Ritz and I, we can open our hotel in Paris next year with no scandal?"

"And I have a complimentary room whenever I wish?"

"*Absolument!* Anything for you, Mademoiselle!" I got the impression that not only was Escoffier agreeable to almost anything Miss Chartier asked, he rather fancied the idea of being under the same roof as her once again, and endeavouring to win her favours through some kind of culinary extravaganza that he had yet to dream up.

"Then our understanding is complete, Auguste."

"*Bien!* And now, I must hasten back to The Savoy Hotel—"

"—where I have no doubt you will hereafter conduct yourself in a professional and ethical manner," suggested Holmes in rather pointed fashion.

"Of course, of course!" Escoffier nodded eagerly. "I do apologise for my past indiscretions and any trouble I may have caused. In fact, bring Miss Adler to The Savoy for a birthday celebration and I shall personally prepare for you the finest feast of your lives."

Miss Adler cast a meaningful glance in the direction of Holmes, "I wouldn't say no to that."

"*Bien!*" Escoffier was clearly anxious to be on his way. "Then I will bid you all a fond *adieu!*"

As he made his way towards our door, one final question for the celebrated chef occurred to me. "I say, in case I'm ever in Paris, do you have a name for this new hotel?"

"Of course! We shall keep it simple. The Ritz!"

With that, Escoffier disappeared even as I felt a kind of befuddled revulsion rising up in the pit of my stomach.

"The Ritz? Is he serious?" I asked. "What kind of egomaniacal buffoon names a hotel after himself?"

Holmes nodded his agreement. "It's a changing world, Watson. There's an East wind coming, to be sure." He then turned to Miss Chartier. "Miss Chartier, if you would be so kind, you will note that the Prince of Wales is still manacled to a serving tray. We wouldn't wish to send him back to Buckingham Palace in such a state, and I don't doubt that you have a key somewhere about your person, so if you would be so kind as to release His Royal Highness, I would be immensely grateful."

"But of course!" Sure enough, Miss Chartier now held a key in her hand. "Now that our business has been concluded in a businesslike fashion."

A moment late Bertie was a free man once again, and gazing at Miss Chartier with what I will diplomatically refer to as admiration.

"You are quite easily the most remarkable woman I have ever met, Miss Chartier. Would you consider a social invitation to Marlborough House?"

Before Miss Chartier could reply, Holmes interceded. "I would advise against that, quite frankly. After all, this isn't the Duchess of Killarney."

"Oh, I see! Yes, she's a commoner. Not of my class."

Hearing a muffled laugh behind me, I turned to see Miss Adler working mightily to suppress a smile. "No, Miss Chartier is definitely in a different class from Your Royal Highness."

"Pity." Bertie gathered up his mask and gloves. "Well, that's that, then. I suppose the British Empire can withstand losing a shiny rock from time to time. Oh, I say, Mr. Holmes. Would you like to be included in the Diamond Jubilee procession tomorrow? Do you like waving?"

"Not particularly," answered Holmes.

"Ah...then may I offer you a knighthood?"

"No, thank you. You're very kind to offer, Bertie, but a knighthood might draw attention to these events and encourage awkward questions."

I cleared my throat, ready to let it be known that I wouldn't be averse to a knighthood, but a sharp glance from Holmes caused the words to die on my lips.

"Point taken," Bertie nodded. "Well then, this has been, I daresay, a most instructive visit..." He seemed inclined to say more, but I could see that his emotions were getting the better of him, and a moment later he wrapped up a very surprised Holmes in a bear hug.

It always amused me whenever anyone aside from Miss Adler embraced Holmes, because it was one of the few situations in which he was utterly at a loss. He would simply stand there, absolutely rigid, enduring it as best he was able, and waiting for it to be over. I sometimes wondered what events in his life had led him to shun any forms of physical affection, and as with most people, I assumed that it had to do with his upbringing. However, this was an area of his life that Holmes never discussed, and I had long ago resigned myself to the fact that, much like the true details surrounding the curious demise of Professor Moriarty, it was destined to remain a mystery.

When Bertie finally released Holmes, he grasped Holmes' hand in his. "I thank you for showing me a future that I could never have imagined for myself before today. I shall hereafter make every effort to conduct myself in a manner befitting my station in life." He then nodded at each one of us in turn. "Miss Adler, Dr. Watson, Miss Chartier..."

Making his way to the door, he pulled his Field Marshal hat from the hat rack and regarded it fondly, then turned to us like a schoolboy who has just found a long-lost toy, "I like hats."

And with those words of wisdom, the future King of England gave a small wave and made his way down our stairs and out into Baker Street. At that point in time, there was no way of knowing if, in fact, the events of the past few hours had made any real impression on him. It's all very well to claim that this or that lesson has been learned in the heat of the moment, but the real test comes in the future as the weeks, months, and years pass. In the case of Bertie, my expectations were not high, but I am happy to say that he confounded them once he became King.

Like many of my fellow countrymen, I feared a continuation of his immature ways and England becoming an embarrassment on the international stage, but to my pleasant surprise he acquitted himself fairly well, particularly in his modernization of the British Home Fleet and reforming the Army after the Second Boer War. No, he did not transform himself into a hero along the lines of Henry V, but he did move from being the ridiculed figure of Tum Tum to becoming Albert Edward, King of England, which was impressive enough in and of itself. What role the little drama that unfolded in our rooms played in this transformation is, of course, open to conjecture, but I do like to think that we played our part in adjusting the path of his life for the better.

Chapter Nine

A Private Conference

Ironically enough, much of Bertie's subsequent redemption once he became King was due to the criminal genius of Marie Chartier, because he would have had no reason to seek out the help of Sherlock Holmes were it not for her elaborate plan to pilfer the Koh-i-Noor Diamond. Having accomplished this with considerable panache, Holmes acknowledged her triumph once Bertie was out of the room.

"Well, Miss Chartier, once again, you have done the Moriarty name proud."

"*Merci*. And once again, it has been an intellectual treat."

"I ask only one favour of you."

"Yes?"

"A simple question. Is that the real Koh-i-Noor Diamond now in your possession, or merely another replica made of glass?"

"A replica, of course. I am not stupid enough to bring the real diamond here."

"As I suspected."

I watched this exchange as I normally did, in my role as both spectator and future chronicler, with Holmes engaging in a few final words with the criminal or client at the heart of the case. In this instance, however, there was something absolutely crucial that I wanted to relate to Holmes, but before I could do that, I was more than a little discomfited to see Miss Chartier turning her attention from Holmes to me.

"And may I ask a favour in return, Mr. Holmes?"

"Of course."

"A moment or two alone with Dr. Watson."

So there it was. I had wondered if she would simply make her good-byes and then disappear into the crowded streets of London. There was no reason that she shouldn't do precisely that, except for the fact that with Miss Chartier, nothing was ever quite as simple as it seemed. This case, to all intents and purposes, had begun with her and I negotiating how we might help one another. With a nice sense of synchronicity and an eye to completing the circle, that was how she wanted the case to end as well.

I was, of course, aware that this was potentially treacherous territory, and I would need to keep all of my wits about me once we were alone. I wondered if she realised just how treacherous it might be for her as well, but that remained to be seen. As Holmes hesitated in replying to Miss Chartier's request, it was Miss Adler who came up with the perfect reason for the two of them to evacuate the premises.

"Darling, I've barely had a bite to eat all day and we just received a personal invitation from Chef Escoffier."

"What are you saying?" responded Holmes. "You want to go to The Savoy Hotel? This minute?"

"If not sooner. I'm absolutely ravenous and it's been ages since I had a decent pheasant."

Holmes hesitated, clearly uncomfortable at the prospect of me being left alone with Miss Chartier. "Will you be all right, Watson?"

"The case is over, my dear," Miss Adler assured him. "Miss Chartier has everything she wants. Dr. Watson is in no danger whatsoever. Now come along..."

Taking Holmes by the hand, Miss Adler led him to the door. With the unsettling prospect of a gourmet meal among the cream of British society only minutes away, Holmes began setting down conditions.

"I'm not singing 'Happy Birthday' in public."

"Of course not," soothed Miss Adler.

"And I'm not eating amphibians of any kind," Holmes continued.

"You needn't worry. If I know Auguste, he will create something completely unique. Who knows, perhaps he'll name a dish after you." Miss Adler opened the door and ushered Holmes through it. "Duck à la Holmes..."

"Stop it."

Miss Adler continued teasing Holmes all the way down the stairs.

"Sherlock Soup..."

"Irene..."

"This is going to be fun!"

"No, no it isn't..."

At length, their voices trailed away. I could feel my heart thumping heavily in my chest as I turned to Miss Chartier and observed her green eyes searching me thoughtfully. For Holmes, Miss Adler, Bertie, and Escoffier, the case was over and they had moved on to other thoughts and activities. However, I knew differently. Whether Miss Chartier knew as well remained to be seen.

I also knew how I hoped the case would ultimately resolve itself, but it would involve getting the better of the quite formidable Miss Chartier, and that was a challenging prospect. Now that we were alone, the die was cast, and as I picked up Holmes' magnifying lens, I determined to let Miss Chartier make the first move. She did not disappoint.

"Well?" she began. "Did you get what I promised you—the greatest Sherlock Holmes story ever?"

"I should say so." This was no exaggeration. All of the elements she had alluded to in her first visit—the Prince of Wales, the greatest chef in the world, and an almost priceless diamond—were the finest ingredients that I could possibly desire. Now all that remained was the last, Escoffier-like touch to make this narrative dish truly sublime. And just like Escoffier, I determined to keep it simple. Taking a steadying breath, I regarded Miss Chartier through the lens, and added the final dash of spice that the recipe required.

"I especially enjoyed your complete fabrication of the murderous Anarchists." Gratified to see a look of apprehension enter Miss Chartier's eyes, I continued. "Come now. It's evident by simply reasoning backwards. There was no Russian bomb-maker, therefore there were never any Anarchists in the empty house across the street, and you weren't hired to assassinate Bertie at all. In fact, his life was never in danger. All you wanted was legal title to the Koh-i-Noor Diamond. May I see the replica?"

I don't believe that I have ever been examined so thoroughly as in the moment it took Miss Chartier to hand me the necklace. She was clearly aware that the sands of the case were shifting beneath her feet, yet felt compelled to play out the story the way she had planned it in her own mind. From the outset, this had been her tale to tell. The characters and plot had been meticulously selected and then set into motion. There would be a beginning, a middle, and then an inevitable end. Ah, but here was where Miss Chartier had made a miscalculation.

As an experienced writer I could have told her as much, as could almost any other writer who has wrestled with putting a story down on paper. Despite all of your plotting and best-laid plans, there are times when characters take on a life of their own. Holmes, Miss Adler, Escoffier, and Bertie had all played their parts as Miss Chartier intended, and were then shuffled off the stage. However, as the final character in her story, I was well aware that I was a character, and I now prepared myself to deviate from her script as I examined the stone beneath the lens.

"Marvellous. Incredible workmanship. Indeed, it's such an authentic replica that there are small specks of dust in the grooves of the mounting, precisely as if it were the genuine article that has been in existence far longer than one week. Since it's worthless, I'm sure you won't mind if I keep it as a souvenir of the case."

As I regarded the glittering bauble and held it up to the light, I now awaited Miss Chartier's next move. She didn't panic, but maintained her cool disposition, merely commenting, "And here I thought it was Mr. Holmes who was the detective." This, as I knew very well, was a delaying tactic, as she considered her new position in all of its implications and adjusted her thinking.

"He is," I replied. "I am merely the storyteller, and I know a good story when I see one. I suspected it would flatter your vanity and sense of occasion to tease Holmes with the real gem, and of course the greatest Sherlock Holmes story ever would not involve a fake, but rather, the one and only Koh-i-Noor Diamond, which is what I now hold in my hand."

"Well done," she remarked, and on cue raised her gun and pointed it at my chest. "But I will take it back now."

And here, I will confess myself a trifle disappointed in Miss Chartier. True, she had just been blindsided by losing the Koh-i-Noor and was improvising as best she could, but a moment's reflection would have told her that all was not as it seemed. In crime, as in so many areas of life, if you are reacting it is too late. The key is to anticipate, which is what I had done only minutes earlier.

"I think not," I replied, and as she proceeded to cock her gun, I was pleased to be able to react as I had seen Holmes do on many previous occasions; that is, with cool disdain bordering on disinterest that conveyed my complete mastery of the situation. It seemed a propitious moment to echo something she had said previously, and so I indulged myself.

"As a wise woman once said, I find that threats made with a gun are infinitely more convincing if the gun actually has bullets in it."

At that, I reached into my pocket, removed the bullets that she imagined to be in her gun, and held them out for her inspection in the palm of my hand. Happily enough, when Miss Chartier had been disarmed earlier, she had given me her gun, and at the first opportunity I made sure that I discreetly unloaded it. She gazed at the bullets in my hand, then lifted her eyes to mine with a laugh.

"Well, well, well...you are simply full of surprises, Dr. Watson."

Having already played out the first part of the scenario in my head, I was not unprepared for what came next. Dropping her gun, she moved with alarming quickness and in a moment had a sword in her hand. She whirled upon me and brandished it with an impressive flourish.

"Then let us see if you find this sword more convincing. Because I am of a sporting disposition, I will give you a moment to get a sword of your own. And then we shall fight a duel for the Koh-i-Noor and add to its bloody history."

Having witnessed Miss Chartier's remarkable fencing ability in "The Adventure of the Elusive Ear," this was not a challenge that I was in any way inclined to accept, and said so. "Most generous of you, Miss Chartier, but no. I have seen you with a sword in your hand, and I don't like my odds."

"Have it your way." As she advanced on me, I like to think that she wasn't intending to actually kill me. I may be wrong on that count, but I sincerely believe that given our history, she had a modicum of respect for me, and if I may flatter myself, perhaps even an ounce or two of affection, to the extent that she was capable of any kind of affection, of course.

No, I imagine that her plan was to encourage me to hand over the Koh-i-Noor with a few well placed, but non-lethal, thrusts and slashes. She would no doubt have succeeded in this had I not foreseen precisely this chain of events. And so as she neared me, I pulled my pepper-pot revolver from my medical bag and aimed it at her. She pulled up short, genuine surprise and dismay on her face for the first time.

"Seriously? What kind of doctor carries a gun in his medical bag?"

"A doctor who accompanies Sherlock Holmes on his cases at a moment's notice."

Gesturing with the gun, she understood my wordless command and proceeded to put the sword down, then turned to me.

"I can see that I underestimated you, Dr. Watson. I have only myself to blame. I judged you not for who you are, but for how you present yourself in your stories. Please accept my apology for suggesting that you were merely a pawn in the world of Sherlock Holmes. You are quite evidently much more than that, and I congratulate you on recovering the Koh-i-Noor Diamond for the British Empire."

"You're very kind," I replied, pleased to have moved up a notch or two in Miss Chartier's estimation.

Shaking her head, she proceeded to sit on the divan, and I must say I felt a twinge of sympathy for her.

"What's the matter?" I asked.

"What's the matter? Have you any idea how much time and planning I put into this? And for what? It was a beautiful, brilliant scheme, and now I walk away completely empty-handed."

"Oh, I wouldn't say that."

"No?"

"You didn't come here merely for me to vouch for you as the Duchess of Killarney. No, you were going to commit the crime of the century, but where is the joy in that if no one knows about it? But here, in the rooms of Sherlock Holmes, with me and my trusty notebook at hand, you knew that every last detail of your criminal genius would be set down for the ages."

For a long moment she considered what I had just said, then nodded, "Perhaps I did. Why should Sherlock Holmes be the only one to have his story told? Without people like me and my father, Sherlock Holmes would not exist. I deserve a chronicler of my own."

"Indeed you do. And I can't tell you how flattered I am that you chose me."

Looking at her from across the room, I calculated just how many potential weapons were within her reach, and upon due consideration, felt safe enough to lower my gun. She regarded me curiously, and for the briefest moment I thought I got a glimpse of the little girl who had grown up as the daughter of

Professor Moriarty. One day, perhaps, I hoped that she would feel comfortable enough with me to share some of her experiences, which I don't doubt were extraordinary in the extreme. For the moment, however, I simply favoured her with what I hope she realised was a genuine smile.

"Sherry?" I offered.

She offered a rueful smile in return. "That would be lovely."

As I poured the two sherries, she leaned back on the divan and took a philosophical view of things. "So that is one round to me, the Post-Impressionist painters, and one round to you, the Koh-i-Noor Diamond."

"I suppose so," I agreed. "Shall we call it a draw then?"

"Of course not. We both play the game for the game's own sake, do we not?"

"That we do," I answered, handing her a glass of sherry.

"And as far as this case is concerned," she continued, "for once you will be able to make yourself the hero in a Sherlock Holmes story."

"Oh no," I demurred. "Were I to write this case up for 'The Strand Magazine,' it would be Sherlock Holmes who recovers the diamond in dramatic fashion. Dr. Watson is merely his assistant and chronicler, after all. I need to make him look good because that's what his devoted readers expect and pay for. However, given the fact that our friend Bertie is central to the story, and considering his lofty position, I'm afraid this particular adventure isn't suitable for 'The Strand.'"

"Of course," she regarded her sherry thoughtfully. "But then, you did say that you wrote up the case with Vincent as 'The Adventure of the Elusive Ear.' May I assume you have similar plans for this story?"

156

"Yes, when a little time passes," I answered. "I think it might be best to allow this tale to marinate for a bit before setting it down on paper for posterity."

"I defer to your good judgement," she said with a smile. "But in getting to know you better, Dr. Watson, there is something that tells me you already know how you will begin this story."

"Perhaps I do."

"Will you share it with me? After all, it is just us two… alone."

And as she gazed at me steadily, all I could do was shake my head. "You're absolutely amazing. A wonder. Unlike any woman I have ever met or ever hope to meet. And you know it. I don't envy the poor men that you set your sights on."

"Don't you?"

"Of course not," I lied. "I am Dr. Watson, after all."

"Of course you are," she agreed. "Now then, tell me how this story begins."

"Hmm...let me see," I began. "Perhaps…'It was in the summer of 1897 and Sherlock Holmes had just left our rooms at 221B Baker Street, when I turned from the window to see a vision beautiful enough to corrupt the soul of any man—the incomparable Marie Chartier had returned...'"

I hoped she would approve of this beginning, and her smile told me that I had succeeded. She lifted her glass.

"...and shall return again."

Clinking our glasses together, we drank to each other, to crime, to a good story, and to her next attempt to get the better of Holmes and I, which would be some years in coming, but all the more memorable when it arrived in the form of Thomas

Edison and Nikola Tesla arriving at 221B to seek our help. But that is a story for another day.

The End.